Highway Robbery

Read all the Carmen Sandiego™ Mysteries:

Highway Robbery

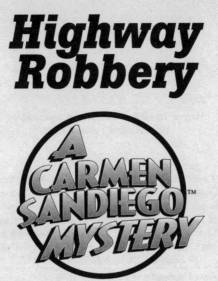

A CARMEN SANDIEGO MYSTERY™

by Bonnie Bader & Tracey West

Illustrated by S. M. Taggart

*Based on the computer software
created by Brøderbund Software, Inc.*

HarperTrophy®
A Division of HarperCollinsPublishers

Highway Robbery

Library of Congress Cataloging-in-Publication Data
Bader, Bonnie 1961–
   Highway robbery / by Bonnie Bader & Tracey West ; illustrated by S. M.
Taggart
      p.   cm.   (A Carmen Sandiego mystery)
   "Based on the computer software created by Brøderbund Software, Inc."
   Summary: When the world's greatest thief causes a national emergency by
stealing Interstate 80, Maya and Ben, the young ACME detectives, set out to
track her down.
   ISBN 0-06-440685-7
   [1. Mystery and detective stories.] I. West, Tracey, 1965– . II. Taggart,
S. M., ill. III. Title. IV. Series.
PZ7.B1377Hi 1997   97-18054
[Fic]—dc21   CIP
                                                                         AC

Typography by Steve Scott
1   2   3   4   5   6   7   8   9   10
❖
First Edition

To Andrea,
who I "shared" the backseat with
on many long car trips!
—B.B.

For Michael and Katie,
who drove me crazy
on family car trips for years.
—T.W.

Prologue
Hackensack, New Jersey

"**A**re we there yet? Are we there yet?" six-year-old Robbie Carter shouted.

His older sister punched him in the arm. "Keep quiet. We haven't even left the driveway."

Sparky, the family mutt, barked loudly from the back of the station wagon.

Robbie leaned over the blue vinyl seat. "Mom, Judy punched me!"

Mrs. Carter was busy struggling with a giant road map. It had started out as a small rectangle. Now it threatened to take over the entire front seat.

"That's nice, Robbie," Mrs. Carter replied.

Robbie's face turned beet red. "Mom! You're not listening!" he whined.

Sparky barked again.

"I only punched him because he is the most annoying person in the entire universe," Judy said, rolling her eyes.

"I am not!" shouted Robbie. He reached over and pinched his sister's leg.

"Ow! Mom, make him stop!" shouted Judy.

"Okay," said Mrs. Carter absentmindedly as she attempted to fold the enormous map.

The driver's door opened. Mr. Carter slid into the front seat. He was wearing an orange tropical shirt, purple shorts, sunglasses, and a straw hat.

"Let's see some smiling faces!" Mr. Carter bellowed. "We're on our way to the vacation of a lifetime! California, here we come!"

"Big deal," Judy muttered.

"I'll pretend I didn't hear that," Mr. Carter said, smiling. He turned the ignition key and backed out of the driveway.

Mrs. Carter frowned. "Don't be so hasty, dear. I need to find something on the map."

Mr. Carter slammed on the brakes, grabbed the map from his wife, and threw it out the window.

"Map, schmap!" he cried. "We don't need no stinkin' map! We're taking Interstate Eighty clear across the continent. No need to take any other road. We'll sail past Pennsylvania's green forests, we'll glide past the cornfields of Nebraska, we'll—"

"We get the picture, Dad," Judy said.

"Arf! Arf!" Sparky barked.

Mr. Carter sighed. "All right, all right, I can take a hint."

"Thank goodness," Judy muttered.

Mr. Carter started driving again. He turned around and grinned at his daughter. "You may be able to stop me from talking about our trip, but you can't stop me from singing! What's a road trip without singing? Come on, everybody: 'California, here we come—'"

"Are we there yet?" Robbie asked again.

Judy grabbed her brother by the collar. "One more word out of you and I'll—"

Mrs. Carter interrupted. "Look, everyone. There's the sign for I-Eighty. We'll be on the highway any minute now."

"Whoopee," Judy said sarcastically.

"Arf! Arf!" Sparky barked.

The station wagon glided onto the on-ramp.

"This is it, kids!" Mr. Carter said. "Our journey is about to begin."

Judy and Robbie started arguing about who was taking up the most room in the backseat. Sparky started howling. Mrs. Carter twisted around in her seat to issue a warning. . . .

Suddenly Mr. Carter slammed on the brakes.

"Honey, what is it?" Mrs. Carter asked, turning around.

Mr. Carter tried to speak but couldn't say a thing. He wordlessly pointed in front of him.

The entire Carter family looked out the front window. A second before, the highway had stretched out before them. But now, where there should have been a highway, there was—nothing. No signs, no lights, no pavement, no painted lines. Just dirt. Dirt as far as the eye could see. And cars stranded everywhere.

Interstate Eighty had vanished into thin air!

The Carter family looked at the scene in front of them in complete silence. For once, no one had anything to say.

Not even Sparky.

1

ACME Headquarters, San Francisco, California

"**I** can't believe it!" Ben muttered. "Fifteen minutes ago we were on our way to the greatest vacation ever. And now we're sitting in The Chief's office. It's not fair."

Maya put her hand on her friend's shoulder. "I'm disappointed too, Ben. I wanted to go to Wonder World more than anything. But if The Chief called us in, it must be important."

"That's right, it *is* important," a stern voice boomed.

Maya and Ben jumped in their seats. They'd know that voice anywhere.

"Sorry, Chief," Ben said, standing up. "I didn't mean to complain. It's just that I was all set to ride

Wonder World's new Chaos Coaster and practice surfing in their simulated beach environment. You know, water and waves without the jellyfish."

"I can see that," The Chief said, eyeing Ben's outfit. He was wearing swim trunks, a T-shirt that said SURF'S UP!, and sandals. His blond hair was covered by a white baseball cap.

Maya stood and walked over to The Chief's desk. "We haven't had a vacation in a long time, Aunt— I mean, Chief," Maya said. Sometimes it was hard to remember that her aunt Velma was head of ACME CrimeNet, the world's greatest crime-fighting organization.

The Chief walked to her desk and sat down. "You're not the only ones who won't be going on vacation this weekend," she said. She pressed a button on her desk and a map on the wall behind her rolled up to reveal a large video monitor. The Chief pressed another button. "Watch this," she said.

Maya and Ben watched as thousands of cars filled the screen. They were all honking. People in the cars were leaning out of their windows and shouting at each other.

Maya let out a low whistle. "That's the worst jam I've ever seen."

"Yeah," Ben said. "I bet those people wish they had some peanut butter to go along with it."

"Very funny," Maya said, rolling her eyes. She turned to The Chief. "What's so special about a traffic jam?"

"This isn't just any traffic jam," The Chief replied. "It's the biggest traffic jam in world history. It looks like this from California all the way to New Jersey."

"Wow!" Maya cried. "That's incredible."

"It sure is," Ben said. "Those cars don't even look like they're on a highway or anything. What happened to the lanes?"

The Chief nodded. "Good observation, gumshoe. You're right. They're not on a highway—but they should be. Those cars started out traveling on Interstate Eighty, the cross-country highway that stretches from New Jersey to California. But sometime today the highway vanished into thin air."

"Carmen!" Maya burst out. Whenever something strange happened, she could be sure that Carmen Sandiego, head of the criminal organization V.I.L.E. (Villains International League of Evil), was behind it somehow.

"I don't get it," Ben said. "I mean, she stole the *T. rex* egg so it would attack ACME headquarters, and the Blarney Stone so everyone would have to tell the truth, but what would Carmen want with a highway?"

Maya was staring into space. She always did that when she was thinking. "I think I know," Maya began. "Highways are really important. Especially a cross-country highway like I-Eighty. People use it to go on vacation, and truckers use it to get goods from one place to another."

Ben took the Ultra-Secret Sender out of his knapsack and began typing furiously. The sender was a combination computer/camcorder/videophone.

"According to the Sender, Interstate Eighty is 2,907 miles long. About 170 million people travel on it every day," Ben said. "It's one of only a few interstate highways that stretch all the way from one coast to the other. No wonder Carmen wants it."

"You're on the right track," The Chief said. "The disappearance of I-Eighty is already causing some big problems. Traffic is completely backed up. Drivers are stranded. And trucking companies are predicting countrywide shortages—everything from produce shortages in New York City to ice-cream shortages in California. The trucks just can't get to their destinations."

Ben looked up from the Sender. "There's more," he said. "Interstate highways make up only one percent of the nation's roads, but they carry twenty percent of the traffic. If Carmen's attacking interstates, the country will be stuck in a permanent jam."

Maya stood up. "It sounds like we'd better get on the case pronto," she said. "Chief, is there any evidence linking Carmen to this?"

The Chief pressed another button. A picture of a small red plane silhouetted against a brilliant blue sky appeared on the video screen.

"Not much. But in the last twenty-four hours, this unidentified aircraft was reported flying from California over Nevada, Utah, Wyoming, Nebraska, Iowa, Illinois . . ."

"Indiana, Ohio, Pennsylvania, and New Jersey!" Ben finished, looking up from the Ultra-Secret Sender. "Those are the states that I-Eighty passes through, right?"

"Affirmative," The Chief said. "We think that one of Carmen's henchpeople was flying that plane, and that he or she had some kind of device that was used to steal the highway."

Ben began typing into the Sender again. "Hey! Maybe they used the shrink ray, like Robin Banks did to shrink the Blarney Stone," he said.

"I don't know," said Maya. "I think they'd need something a lot more powerful. Maybe they came up with something new." She turned to The Chief. "So what do you want us to do?"

The Chief pressed another button, and a road map of the United States appeared on the screen. Interstate Eighty was outlined in red. There was a big red X over New Jersey.

"The V.I.L.E. plane was last seen in New Jersey, where I-Eighty begins," she said.

"Or ends!" Ben interrupted. The Chief gave him a look. "D-d-depending on where you're coming from, right, Chief?" he stammered.

The Chief sighed. "Correct, gumshoe. As I was saying, I'll be sending you two on a private ACME jet to New Jersey. You can begin searching for clues there."

"New Jersey!" Ben groaned. "I guess I shouldn't bother bringing my surfboard."

Maya laughed. "Actually, New Jersey is famous for its beaches," she said. "Ever hear of the Jersey shore? But something tells me we won't have time for surfing."

"Correct once again," The Chief replied. She pressed a button, and a picture of a woman who looked to be in her early sixties flashed on the screen. Her gray hair hung in a long braid. She wore a bandanna around her neck, a black leather jacket, and a T-shirt that read ROAD WARRIOR.

"Who's that?" Ben asked. "V.I.L.E.'s newest criminal? She looks pretty dangerous."

The Chief smiled. "This time you're wrong, Ben. That 'criminal' is one of ACME's most trusted friends. Her name is Dusty Rhoads. She used to drive a tour bus for a rock band. She'll pick you up at Newark Airport in New Jersey and take you wherever you need to go."

Ben gulped. "Couldn't we get somebody a little—safer-looking?"

"She's the best in the business," The Chief snapped. "And with Interstate Eighty out of commission, you'll need someone who knows her way around smaller highways and back roads."

"Whatever you say, Chief," Ben said. Under his breath he muttered, "Well, it was nice knowing you!"

"Ben!" Maya shouted.

"I know, I know, I need a better attitude," Ben said.

"No, not that!" Maya said. She pointed to the screen. "Look!"

The screen went staticky, and Dusty Rhoads's picture disappeared. Then another woman came into focus. She wore a red cloak, and dark hair spilled out from under a red fedora. The hat was pulled down to cover her face.

"Carmen!" they all cried at once.

"That's right, gumshoes. Carmen here," the master criminal purred. "I have a special message for you, Chief. One of my agents has stolen Interstate Eighty."

"We already figured that out!" Ben shouted.

Carmen ignored him. "And I will destroy I-Eighty seven days from now. Unless . . ."

"Unless what?" The Chief snapped. "I don't bargain with criminals, Carmen."

Carmen laughed. "Oh, but you will. Have you seen the traffic jams? Have you seen the disappointed faces of kids whose vacations have been ruined? The country can't function without I-Eighty. And I will destroy it. Unless you resign as head of ACME and come work for me at V.I.L.E."

"Never!" The Chief thundered.

"You have seven days," Carmen replied, "or I will keep my promise, and turn Interstate Eighty into a pile of dust. You can count on that."

The screen went black.

2
Newark, New Jersey

Maya and Ben sank into their seats.

"The Chief, work for Carmen?" Ben shouted. "Never!" He whipped off his baseball cap and threw it down on The Chief's desk. It skidded across the desk and landed on the floor.

"Take it easy, gumshoe," The Chief said, picking up the hat and handing it back to Ben. "That will never happen." She began to pace back and forth in front of the screen where Carmen's image had appeared only moments before.

"Especially not with us on the case," Maya added. "Right, Chief?"

"That's right, Maya," The Chief replied. She stopped pacing and faced Maya and Ben. "You two have come very close to catching Carmen time and time again. That is precisely why I called you in for this case. Although I didn't count on Carmen's ultimatum." The Chief ran her hand through her short, dark hair.

"Well, we have seven days," Maya said, jumping to her feet. "Let's get to work!" She grabbed Ben's cap from his hand and slapped it on his head.

"Ouch!" Ben cried, rubbing his head.

Maya laughed. "Hey, if you were surfing right now, those waves would be smacking you a lot harder!"

Ben rolled his eyes. "Thanks for reminding me again about what I'm missing."

"Ahem!" The Chief glared at Maya and Ben. "We have work to do here!" she said.

"Sorry, Chief," Maya said, looking a bit embarrassed. She knew that this was a big case—their biggest one yet—and she was anxious to get to work.

"Are we still going to fly to New Jersey?" Maya asked, getting back to business.

"That was the plan," The Chief said. "Do you have another suggestion?"

Maya and Ben both shook their heads.

"Well, good luck, gumshoes," The Chief said.

"My future as the head of ACME depends on your success."

Maya and Ben took deep breaths and looked at each other. Ben broke the silence.

"New Jersey, here we come!" And with that, they headed out to the plane.

"What's the matter, Ben? Feeling a little airsick?" Maya asked as the plane hit some turbulence.

Ben picked up a spoon from his tray and looked at his reflection. He could see that his face did look a bit green, even upside down. But he wasn't feeling sick because of the plane ride; he was feeling sick over this case. "I was just thinking about what Carmen said," Ben explained.

"I know what you mean, Ben," Maya said. "Carmen's really done it this time. But don't worry, we'll track down Carmen's henchperson and return Interstate Eighty before the seven days are up, right?"

"I guess so," Ben said.

Maya punched Ben in the arm. "What do you mean 'I guess so'? Of *course* we will!"

Ben rubbed his arm and smiled. "Let's review the clues we have so far." He grabbed the Ultra-Secret Sender, flipped it open, and began typing.

Maya looked over his shoulder and read:

CASE FILE: THEFT OF INTERSTATE EIGHTY.

LOCATION OF CRIME: THE UNITED STATES,

FROM NEW JERSEY TO CALIFORNIA.

SUSPECTS:

Ben stopped typing and looked up. "What do you think?" he asked Maya.

Maya thought for a moment. "Well, The Chief told us that someone spotted a small red plane."

"So for starters, let's get a list of all the V.I.L.E. agents who have a pilot's license," Ben suggested. He typed the information into the Sender and read:

HAMMOND SWISS. BLOND HAIR, GREEN EYES.

HOBBY: PAINTING. FOOD: DIETETIC.

SPORT: SKIING. MUSIC: CLASSICAL.

POLLY GRAPH. RED HAIR, GREEN EYES.

HOBBY: CARD GAMES. FOOD: DIETETIC.

SPORT: BOWLING. MUSIC: CLASSICAL.

MAE HEMM. RED HAIR, GRAY EYES.

HOBBY: CARD GAMES. FOOD: VEGETARIAN.

SPORT: DANCING. MUSIC: SALSA.

RAY ZARUMPUS. BROWN HAIR, BROWN EYES.

HOBBY: CARD GAMES. FOOD: FRENCH.

17

SPORT: DANCING. MUSIC: SALSA.

RHETT BARRON. BLOND HAIR, GREEN EYES.

HOBBY: STAMP COLLECTING. FOOD: ITALIAN.

SPORT: SKIING. MUSIC: ROCK.

"Fasten your seat belts, kids," the pilot called out. "We're about to land."

Maya fastened her belt, leaned her head back on the soft leather headrest, and closed her eyes. She thought about their other cases and how Carmen had eluded Ben and her each time. They had always come so close, but somehow Carmen managed to slip away time and time again. *Not this case,* Maya promised herself. *This time we won't let her get away!*

"Hey, what's with the crowds?" Ben asked once they had landed and were walking through Newark Airport. "I've never seen so many people in one place before! Do you think the airlines are running some sort of major sale or something?"

"Earth to Ben," Maya said. "Remember the case we're working on? People can't *drive* to their destinations, so they're *flying* there."

Ben blushed. "Oh, yeah, I was just—*oof!*" Ben collided with a woman who was rushing through the airport in the opposite direction.

18

Hammond Swiss

Polly Graph

Mae Hemm

Ray Zarumpus

Rhett Barron

"Cool duds," the woman said to Ben. "Are you a surfer dude or something?"

Ben looked down at his clothes. In all the excitement at ACME headquarters, he had forgotten to change out of his surfing outfit. Ben looked up at the woman. She looked vaguely familiar. But who *was* she?

"Dusty?" Maya asked.

"Oh, you must be Dusty Driver, our road . . . I—I mean Dusty Rhoads, our driver," Ben said, blushing again.

Dusty laughed. The silver chains on her black leather jacket rattled. Ben took a closer look at her. She looked exactly the same as she did in the profile The Chief had shown them.

Dusty flipped her long braid over her shoulder. She stuck out her hand and said, "Pleased to meet you, little detectives. Dusty Rhoads, at your service."

Ben stuck out his hand to shake. But instead of giving him an ordinary handshake, Dusty slapped his hand, grabbed it, squeezed it, slapped it again, pulled his fingers, then lifted his hand into the air. It all happened so fast that Ben could barely catch his breath.

Maya watched the proceedings very closely.

She stuck out her hand, but instead of being confused like Ben, Maya was able to follow Dusty's every move.

"All right, gumshoe girl!" Dusty said with a grin.

Ben shook his head. *Is that some sort of secret handshake?* he wondered.

"Whatcha waiting for, surfer boy?" Dusty said. "It's time for a powwow."

"Powwow?" asked Ben

"Yeah, I used to live on a reservation a couple of years ago," she said with a shrug, as she led them to the waiting area. "Anyway, while I was waiting for your plane to land, I started doing a little detective work. It turns out the agent abandoned the plane here. I found an eyewitness, but he wanted to tell his story to someone with proper ACME credentials, so I told him to meet us here."

"Cool," said Maya. "Well, while we're waiting, I just have to say that this is one case that just doesn't add up. If Carmen's agent had a plane, why didn't he or she just fly to the rendezvous with Carmen? Why abandon the plane?"

"That's a good question, Maya," Ben said. "Hopefully we'll get some answers from this mystery eyewitness."

21

"And here I am," said a voice. "But where are the ACME agents?"

Maya and Ben turned around and saw a young man in a steward's uniform. He looked at Maya and Ben quizzically.

Ben stood up as tall as he could and said, "We *are* ACME agents, sir," and showed him his credentials. Maya did the same.

"Sorry," the steward said sheepishly. "I just wasn't expecting you to be kids." He reached out and shook their hands. Ben was happy to find he used the more traditional handshake.

"I'm Stuart, by the way, and I'd be glad to tell you my story."

Maya and Ben looked at him expectantly.

"We had just landed flight 626 from Albuquerque when I noticed a small red plane on the runway. I said to myself, 'Stuart, that plane is not a commercial liner, and it does not belong on this airstrip.' The next thing I knew, two air control officers approached the plane. All of a sudden there was smoke everywhere. When it cleared, the plane was empty and a courtesy van was missing!"

Ben whistled softly. "Carmen's agent must have used the quick-escape-by-smoke-bomb trick. It's an oldie but a goodie."

"Can we see the plane?" Maya asked.

"I don't think that will be a problem," said Stuart. "Come right this way."

He led the three of them down a hallway and through an exit door. The plane stood nearby. Maya and Ben climbed aboard and began their search.

"Well, he or she definitely had a small but powerful machine to shrink that highway. There isn't room in this plane for much else besides the pilot," said Ben.

They went over the cockpit with a fine-tooth comb, but there was nothing—not a single tiny clue—to be found.

Maya sat in the pilot's seat and stared dejectedly at the controls. Suddenly she noticed something. "Hey, look," she said. "The gas gauge is on E. That explains why the agent stopped here."

"Yeah," Ben agreed. "It makes sense. The agent must have been on his or her way to deliver the road to Carmen, when he or she ran out of gas. When they landed the plane and the officers came over to investigate, the thief escaped. That must have put Carmen's plans into a tailspin. The only question is, where was the plane going?"

Maya took one final look around the cockpit. "Well, there certainly aren't any clues here." She and Ben left the plane and joined Dusty and Stuart.

"Hey, did you guys find anything?" Dusty wanted to know.

"No such luck." Maya sighed. "I just can't believe there are no clues to be found. How disappointing."

"Hey, I just thought of something!" Ben shouted. "Where was the van that the agent stole? Maybe he or she dropped something in the rush to steal it."

"Good thinking, Ben!" Maya said as Stuart led them to the corner of the airfield where the vans were kept.

"It was parked right here," Stuart said. "It was a red van used to drive passengers to the smaller planes."

"A *red* van," said Maya. "It figures."

But there were no clues on the ground anywhere near the van's parking spot.

"Hey, guys, what about that?" Ben suddenly said, pointing to a nearby garbage can. "Maybe the agent disposed of the evidence."

"Ben, you're a genius!" said Maya.

She and Ben ran over to the can and peered into it. Stuart and Dusty followed.

Stuart leaned over, got a whiff, and held his

nose. "Good luck," he said in a
"It's time for flight 1205 to Wall.
run."

"Thanks for your help!" Maya call

The two gumshoes eyed the garbage
Wasps buzzed around the top of it. The s___ was
truly unbearable.

"I'll flip ya," Maya said.

"Oh, no, I wouldn't think of it," Ben replied
gallantly. "Ladies first."

Dusty sighed and pulled a pair of black leather
motorcycle gloves out of her pocket. "Out of the
way, dudes. I'm going in."

She reached into the can and pulled out a rotten
banana peel, an old pizza box, and a fried-chicken
bucket.

"Why don't you check these things out before
I stick my hands in there again," she said.

The pizza box was empty, as was the chicken
bucket. The rotten banana skin was just, well,
rotten. But then Maya took a second look. "Hey,
I think I see a piece of paper," she said.

She reached inside the chicken bucket and
picked it up.

"Does it say anything?" asked Ben.

"'If you're not big into fried chicken, you know

to meet me,'" she read. "Hey—the words
g and *chicken* are underlined. What do you think
that means?"

"I'm not sure," Ben said. "Maybe it's a clue to
where the agent is supposed to meet Carmen. But
it doesn't really help us—it could be anywhere in
the United States!"

"Let's head over to the bus, guys," said Dusty.
"We can put our heads together once we get settled."

Maya pocketed the clue, and the band of three
headed to the short-term parking lot. They had a
lot of thinking to do.

I am Carmen Sandiego, the greatest thief the world has ever known. And I don't like it—not one bit— when things don't go as planned. That highway should already be in my hands. But my agent was forced to abandon our original plan and take a much slower route. My agent will never make it to our assigned rendezvous in time. But they say that necessity is the mother of invention, and they are correct. I, the most devious criminal mind ever, have come up with a brilliant backup plan—a little cross-country cat-and-mouse game. Those gum-shoes will be lost in no time. And then Interstate Eighty—and The Chief—will be mine!

3
New Jersey Turnpike, Exit 13

Ben and Maya stood inside Dusty's RV, looking around in amazement.

"Cool," said Ben.

"Very cool," said Maya.

It was an old tour bus, completely customized inside. There was a living room, a kitchen, a bathroom, and bunks in the back. If they had to hit the road, at least they'd be riding in comfort.

"Anyone have a suggestion about which way we should go?" Dusty asked.

"Sorry, Dusty," said Maya. "Our clue is not very specific at all. Do you have any ideas, Ben?"

"Hmm," Ben said. He was busy typing information into the Ultra-Secret Sender.

"What are you up to?" Maya asked.

"If my memory serves me right," Ben said, "ACME has an informant who works as a toll taker on the New Jersey Turnpike." He continued typing.

"All right!" said Maya. "Maybe he or she has seen something that could help us out with this chicken clue."

"Bingo!" Ben shouted. "Here it is. Tina Tolltaker—ACME informant. And today she's working the third lane at exit thirteen."

Dusty scrambled to the driver's seat, and they were off. A short time later, they pulled up to Tina's booth.

Maya leaned across Dusty, stuck her head out the window, and flashed her ACME badge.

Tina looked around, then nodded. "How can I help you?" she asked Maya.

"We're on a case, Tina. A big one," Maya began. "Have you seen any suspicious activity lately? Particularly involving a red van?"

"You know nothing gets by Tina. Nothing. I see all!" she said.

"What is it?" Maya asked anxiously.

"Aside from tons more traffic than usual? Well, a little while ago, a red van with darkened windows pulled up. The driver rolled down the window just a crack—left just enough space to slip the ticket out to me," Tina said, waving a toll ticket.

"Now, I found that strange," she said, her eyes darting back and forth. "Mighty strange. I always get a look at the driver's face. A good look. Why, just yesterday, I saw the strangest-looking fellow. He was—"

"Tina," Maya interrupted. "Please get back to the red van."

"Oh, yes," Tina said, snapping to attention. "Anyway, just as I thought the van was about to pull away, the driver rolled down the window again and croaked, 'The Peach State or bust!'"

"Peach State!" Maya shouted with glee. "That's Georgia!"

"Excellent," said Dusty. "Thanks for your help, Tina."

Tina smiled. "I just had an idea," she said. "Why don't I notify my other toll-taker and road-side-crew friends down South that you're on the lookout for a red van. If I pick up any info, I'll fax it to you!"

"That'll be great!" Maya said. She handed Tina a card with their fax number, and they sped off.

Georgia! Ben bent his head over the Ultra-Secret Sender. "I'm looking for chicken in Georgia.

There are still so many possibilities."

"Hey, how about a *big* chicken in Georgia," Maya suggested.

A couple of seconds later Ben hit pay dirt. "All right! I found it—the Big Chicken!" he said.

"Dusty!" he called out. "Next stop, Marietta, Georgia!"

"Cool!" Dusty shouted. "We're ready to roll!"

4
Marietta, Georgia →
Petal, Mississippi

Ben had a big map open. "I'm trying to plot out Dusty's route. It looks like we should take—"

"Let's leave the driving to Dusty," Maya interrupted. "But while you're spouting off information, why don't you give me some info on Georgia?"

"Sure," Ben said, flipping the Sender open. "'Georgia is the largest state east of the Mississippi River,'" he read. "'It was the last of the original thirteen colonies to be founded, in 1733. Georgia is bordered on the north by Tennessee and North Carolina, on the east by South Carolina and the Atlantic Ocean, on the south by Florida, and on the west by Alabama. The capital and largest city is Atlanta, host of the 1996 Summer Olympics. Among the farm products that are produced in Georgia are peaches, peanuts, cattle, eggs, and broilers.'"

"There must be some pretty huge broilers," Maya joked, thinking about the big chicken they were headed to see.

Ben laughed and rubbed his eyes. "If you don't mind, Maya," he said, "I'm beat. I really need to go to sleep."

Maya jumped up and ran to the back of the bus. "I get the top bunk!" she called.

Fifteen hours later, Dusty pulled the bus up to the Big Chicken on Cobb Parkway in Marietta, Georgia. It sat on top of a fast-food chicken restaurant.

"Well, I don't see a red van anywhere," Ben said. "Maybe we're too late."

"Or maybe the henchperson parked the van out of sight," Maya said. "I think we need to take a look around."

Ben and Maya hopped off the bus. A huge metal chicken loomed before them. Crowds of people stood around, gawking at the monstrosity.

Maya pulled out the information on the Big Chicken. "It says here that the Chicken is often used as a landmark for directions for highway travelers and aircraft." Maya looked up at the big bird. Its huge eyes rolled around, and its gigantic beak opened and shut.

"It looks like it's trying to say something!" Maya said, pointing at the chicken.

"It's probably saying, 'Get me out of this heat!'" Ben replied, wiping sweat from his brow.

"Well, we are in the South, after all," Maya said. "And depending on where this case takes us, it might only end up getting hotter."

Ben groaned. "Well, let's get inside where there's air-conditioning," he said.

There were even more people inside the restaurant than there were outside. Maya walked up to a plaque on the wall and read some information about the Chicken.

"Can you believe that the Chicken is fifty-five feet tall? That's about five stories high!" she told Ben.

"Where did it come from?" Ben asked.

"It says here that the Chicken was built in 1963 to advertise Johnny Reb's Chick, Chuck and Shake. Kentucky Fried Chicken bought it later," Maya said.

"And check this out," she added with a chuckle. "In 1993 a windstorm came, ruffled the chicken's sheet metal feathers, and plucked the big bird naked!"

"And let me guess what happened next," Ben said. "They knit a huge sweater for the bird to keep it warm!"

"Very funny," said Maya. "Actually, a huge 'Save the Chicken' campaign was started, and after receiving almost ten thousand calls, Kentucky Fried Chicken decided to restore the bird."

"Good thing," replied Ben. "I guess they didn't want to have a chicken riot on their hands!"

Maya rolled her eyes. "Come on," she said. "Let's have a look around."

Maya pushed her way through the crowds, searching for either the henchperson or a clue. She shook her head as she scanned the faces. People were snapping pictures and buying souvenirs—T-shirts, hats, pins—all to commemorate the fact that they had seen the Big Chicken.

Maya walked over to a counter covered with booklets. She picked up information about other tourist attractions in Georgia: Centennial Park (built for the Olympics) in Atlanta; and Stone Mountain, which features huge figures of Jefferson Davis and Confederate generals Lee and Jackson

carved into the mountainside.

"See anything strange around here lately?" Maya asked the woman behind the counter, after she had flashed her badge.

"Nothing stranger than usual," the woman said in a friendly Southern accent. "I do work under a fifty-five-foot chicken, you know."

Maya was feeling a little desperate. "Anything at all would help," she said.

The woman furrowed her brow in thought. "Well," she said, after a moment. "This morning, when I came into work, there was a note from the night cashier that a woman in red came in last night, bought one of our guidebooks, scribbled something in it, and said to give that very book to a person in a black coat."

"Carmen!" Maya said. "And did this person in the black coat come in?"

"Yes, just a little while ago," the woman replied.

"Did you get a good look at the person?"

"Not really," the woman said. "The person had on dark glasses and a hat, so I couldn't even tell if it was a man or a woman. But I'll tell you one thing—the person never even said thank you! I guess they don't believe in Southern hospitality."

"Two more questions," Maya said. "Number one, which guidebook was it, and number two, did you happen to see what the woman in red wrote in it?"

The woman handed Maya a guidebook entitled *Everything You've Always Wanted to Know About Roadside Attractions but Were Afraid to Ask.* Maya thought, *Hmm, this is strange.*

The woman was thinking hard. "She wrote . . . I think it was . . ."

Maya held her breath.

"I remember! 'Put the pedal to the metal'!" she said happily.

"'Put the pedal to the metal'?" Maya repeated. What did *that* mean?

"Wait a minute—there was something else— oh, that's right. It was very strange. Instead of 'pedal' it was spelled p-e-t-a-l. Like a flower," the woman said. "That woman in red must be a pretty bad speller!"

Perhaps, thought Maya. *Or maybe it's a clue!*

Maya paid for the guidebook and thanked the woman for her help.

"Oh, anytime," the woman replied. "Y'all come back now, y'hear?"

Maya stepped outside and found Ben. He had

a huge bucket of chicken in his hands and was munching on a drumstick.

"Get anything?" he asked.

"I think so," said Maya. "How about you?"

"Well, the counterperson remembered a suspicious-looking person in a black coat, a hat, and sunglasses, ordering fried chicken. How about you?"

Maya filled him in on the information she had received.

"It sounds like something Dusty would say," Ben said.

"Except for the spelling," Maya said.

She entered the info into the Ultra-Secret Sender. "Check it out, Ben—*petal* could mean Petal, Mississippi. I have an idea—this book might come in handy." She flipped to the index. "Here it is—Petal, Mississippi, the International Checker Hall of Fame. This henchperson must really be into some weird roadside attractions!"

Maya and Ben stepped onto the bus.

"Dusty!" Ben called out. "Next stop—Petal, Mississippi."

"Sure thing!" She zoomed off.

Maya and Ben settled down to rest. "Petal is about three hundred and fifty miles southwest of here," Maya said. "We should be there in about six hours. Hand me a piece of that chicken, Ben."

Ben slapped himself in the head. "I think we've overlooked a clue, Maya. The counterperson told me the henchperson ordered chicken." Ben called up the list of suspects on the Sender.

"Well, we can definitely eliminate one suspect," he reported. "Mae Hemm is a vegetarian."

"And what about Hammond Swiss and Polly Graph?" Maya asked. "They eat dietetic food. And fried chicken isn't exactly dietetic."

Ben shrugged. "Maybe they ate it without the skin," he suggested.

"You're right," Maya said. "We don't have enough to eliminate those two right now."

"Let's get some info on this Checker Hall of Fame place," Ben suggested.

This time Maya read the information: "'Players from around the world come to Petal to participate in international checker tournaments. People also come for state, regional, and national matches.' And check this out," Maya said. "This place was created by Charles Walker, a self-made millionaire and former checkers champ who put up one million dollars to build the place."

Maya looked over at Ben for a reaction. But

he was fast asleep. Maya thought that looked like a good idea, and closed her eyes too.

About six hours later, Dusty pulled the bus into the small town of Petal, Mississippi. "Rise and shine!" she called to Ben and Maya. "We're here!"

Ben stretched and stood up. His body felt stiff— but no wonder. He had spent the past six hours sleeping in a chair. He couldn't wait to get outside, even though it was hot and humid.

When he got off the bus, a gigantic Tudor building loomed before him. His eyes scanned the building, and he noticed a seven-story tower on top. The grounds surrounding the building appeared endless, and they were dotted with what looked like mini-estates.

"Come on, Maya," Ben called. "Let's check this place out."

Maya rubbed her eyes and stepped off the bus. The air was hot and humid.

Once inside the building, Maya and Ben found a huge checkerboard, complete with pieces, on the basement floor of the tower.

Ben let out a low whistle. "I've never seen anything like that before." He looked up. There was even a checkerboard on the ceiling!

"Pretty impressive, huh?" a voice called out.

Maya and Ben looked up and saw a man standing on a balcony above the checkerboard. "That playing area is 256 square feet," the man told them.

"Do they really play on that?" Ben wanted to know. "I mean, it seems it would be pretty hard to concentrate."

The man laughed. "No, young man. The players sit at those tables, and someone else stands on the floor simulating their moves."

Ben walked over to the tables. "Very cool!" he said.

"Would you two care to play a game?" the man asked. "Things are a little slow around here today."

Maya glared at Ben. She knew that he was probably *dying* to play, but they had work to do.

"Hey, you!" the man called out suddenly. "What do you think you're doing?"

Maya and Ben turned around and saw a figure lifting up one of the huge checker pieces from the board. The piece covered the person's face, so that only a long black coat was visible.

A long black coat? Maya thought, remembering what the woman had told her at their last stop. "That's the agent!" she cried out, charging ahead.

Maya ran across the checkerboard. But as soon

as she neared the henchperson, a giant checker piece came flying at her!

"Watch out, Maya!" Ben tried to push her out of the way, but he was too late. The checker piece slammed into Maya's head, knocking her to the ground.

"Are you okay?" Ben asked, rushing up to her.

Maya rubbed her head. "I'm fine. It was just a pillow."

"A pillow?" Ben asked, touching the red cushion.

"Come on, Ben," Maya said. "The agent is getting away!" Maya jumped up and raced out of the room.

She saw a flash of black ahead of her. "This way, Ben!" she shouted. She ran into a room, but it was empty. "I could have sworn the agent went this way!" she exclaimed.

"He probably did," said a voice. Maya turned around. It was the man who had been standing on the balcony. "But this place is filled with secret passages. You'll never find who you were after now! By the way, what is going on?"

"I'm sorry, sir," Maya said. "We have no time to explain."

Maya and Ben ran out of the building to the

bus. But the bus was gone! "Great time for Dusty to go on a road trip!" Maya said, kicking the dirt. "Now we're really doomed. We don't even have a clue as to where to go next."

Just then the bus pulled up. Dusty opened the door. "Sorry, guys," she said. "I was chilling on the lawn when this figure dressed in black zoomed past me and jumped into a red van. I was sure it was the same van Tina Tolltaker told us about, so I took off after it."

"And?" Maya asked.

"Got pulled over for a speeding ticket. And wouldn't you know it, the red van got off scot-free!"

"Did the henchperson say or do anything unusual?" Ben asked, fishing for clues.

"All I heard was 'Gotta hop to it! Hop to it! Hop, hop, hop!'" Dusty said.

"That has to be a clue," Maya said, pulling out the roadside-attractions guide. "Now, what hops?"

"A grasshopper?" suggested Dusty.

"A rabbit?" said Ben, looking up from the Ultra-Secret Sender. "There's a town called Rabbit in Nebraska."

"Maybe," said Maya. "But I've got something here too. In Eureka Springs, Arkansas, there's a museum entirely filled with frogs. Frogs hop too."

Ben sighed. "They both sound like possibilities. What should we do?"

The Ultra-Secret Sender whirred. A sheet of paper shot out of the fax-machine port.

"It's from Tina Tolltaker," Ben said. "It says, 'Red van spotted at toll booth in Mississippi. Driver asked for directions to Ozark Mountains.'"

"That's our answer!" Maya cried. "The Ozark Mountains cross the northwest section of Arkansas."

Maya turned to Dusty and smiled. "Frog Fantasies Museum, here we come!"

5
Eureka Springs, Arkansas

"**I** can't wait until we get to the frog museum," Ben said. He took a long, squeaky sip through his soda straw.

"Ben, there's nothing left in that cup," Maya said. "It's been two hours since we stopped at that drive-through catfish place near Jackson, Mississippi."

Ben licked his lips. "Mmm, that sure was a delicious dinner. I never knew hush puppies tasted so good. I always thought they were shoes."

Dusty's laugh rang out from the driver's seat. "Hush puppies are balls of fried corn bread. A real Southern delicacy."

Maya walked up to Dusty's seat. "Do you like Southern food?"

"Sure do," Dusty said. "I always liked driving through the South. There's some real beautiful country out here. Especially where we're going."

"Have you been to Eureka Springs before?" Maya asked.

Dusty nodded. "In the late seventies I was touring with the Strolling Gnomes. They had a gig in Little Rock, and a local sax player jammed with us. His name was Bill. After the show, he took us up by Eureka Springs. Said he was born around there. It's in the foothills of the Ozark Mountains, and there are hundreds of natural hot springs there."

Maya stared at Dusty in surprise. "A saxophone player named Bill from Arkansas? Do you mean President Clinton? He grew up in a town called Hot Springs."

Dusty winked. "My memory's not what it used to be, but anything's possible, right?"

Ben flipped through the roadside-attractions guidebook. "Eureka Springs sounds nice, but I really want to know more about this museum."

Maya looked over his shoulder. "It sure sounds strange. I mean, who would want to start a museum of frogs?"

Ben pointed to a page. "It says here the

47

museum opened in the 1950s. A woman named Louise Mesa and her family had a huge collection of all kinds of frog things—toys, statues, jewelry, and stuff. So she and her husband built a special room in their house and opened up a frog museum."

"How many frogs are there?" Maya asked.

"Six thousand!" Ben said. "That doesn't count the real frogs that live in a pond behind the house."

Maya smiled. "It sounds like things are really jumping at that place!"

Dusty turned around from the front seat. "I hate to interrupt your discussion, dudes," she said. "But I thought you might want to check out the view."

Maya and Ben hurried to the windows. In the north, they could see the tops of tall hills, bathed in pink light by the setting sun.

"The Ozarks!" Maya cried. "They really are beautiful."

"I'll say," Ben said. "That means we're getting closer to the frog museum."

"Good call, dude," Dusty said. "I'll take back roads to state highway Twenty-three. It will add a few miles, but we'll avoid the traffic jam on Interstate Forty. We'll go through the Ozark Forest, through the mountains, and straight into Eureka Springs. We'll be there in about three hours."

"We're here!"

Maya woke to the sound of Dusty's voice. The sky was pitch black. Across from her, Ben was rubbing his eyes.

"We must have taken a nap," Maya said. She looked at the dashboard. The digital clock read 11:00.

"We're right on schedule," Dusty said. "But it doesn't look like our schedule and the museum's are the same." She pointed outside the window.

A three-story stone house stood in front of them. A wooden sign on the front door read FROG FANTASIES MUSEUM AND GIFT SHOP. Tall evergreens loomed behind the house.

"According to the book, Louise Mesa lives in the top part of the house," Ben said.

"That may be so, but the lights are off and the driveway is empty," Maya said. "It doesn't look like anyone's home."

Ben shrugged. "We should still check the grounds. Carmen's agent can't be too far ahead of us."

"You're right," Maya said. "Let's go."

"I'm going to stay here and see if I can locate a place in my Arkansas guidebook for us to camp tonight," Dusty said. "But I'll keep an eye on you guys."

A full moon lit the path in front of them as Maya and Ben walked to the house.

"Look," Ben whispered. "The door's open a crack. Maybe the henchperson's inside."

Maya frowned. "Are you sure it's okay to go in?"

"It's a national emergency!" Ben hissed. "I don't think anyone would mind."

Maya nodded. "You're right, Ben. Let's go."

The door creaked as Maya and Ben stepped inside.

"Leaping amphibians!" Ben said. He let out a low whistle. "It's raining frogs and—frogs!"

The bright moonlight lit up the walls of the museum. Thousands upon thousands of frogs, with their large black eyeballs, stared at Maya and Ben.

"This is amazing," Maya said. "There are dancing frogs, and singing frogs, and frogs on surfboards—"

"And wooden frogs, and silver frogs, and china frogs," Ben said. "This place is un-*frog*-gettable!"

Maya groaned, then suddenly tensed. "Did you hear that?"

"Hear what?" Ben asked.

"I heard a noise—like a croak," Maya said.

Ben's eyes lit up. "It must be the frog pond out back!" he said. "Let's check it out."

Maya and Ben walked past the frogs and out the back door. A small pond sat in the middle of the backyard.

"I don't hear anything," Maya said, peering at the dark water. "These frogs must be asleep."

A loud croak traveled through the night air.

"I definitely heard that," Ben said. "But it's not coming from the pond."

Maya pointed to the trees behind them. "It's coming from back there."

As Maya and Ben walked toward the trees, the croaking grew louder and louder.

Suddenly Maya bent down. "Take a look at this!" she said, holding up a tape recorder. She pressed the off button, and the croaking stopped. "Here's our frog."

"It must be some kind of trick," Ben said. "We'd better get Dusty."

"Good idea," Maya said. She started to run— and nearly fell on her face.

"I—I can't move!" she cried. "My feet are stuck!"

"Mine too," Ben said. "It looks like we've landed on flypaper."

"A trap!" Maya groaned. "What will we do?"

Ben took a pen-sized flashlight from his pocket and shone it on the ground. "Carmen's agent used a huge piece of flypaper to trap us. If we can untie our sneakers, maybe we can—"

"I know!" Maya said excitedly. "We've just got to make like frogs—and jump! If we jump far enough, we'll land on dirt, and not flypaper."

"Let's hop to it!" Ben cried. "I'll try it first."

Ben wiggled out of his sneakers, jumped as far as he could, and landed on his knees safely in the dirt. Maya almost landed on top of him.

"We did it!" Maya cried.

"Let's take one more look inside before we go back to the van," Ben said. "We may have missed something."

They ran back into the frog museum, past the rows and rows of frogs. Suddenly Maya stopped in her tracks.

"Ben," she whispered. "Come and look at this."

On a shelf, twenty green porcelain frogs were lined up in a neat row. At the end of the row sat one more porcelain figure, but it wasn't green—and it wasn't a frog.

"A white squirrel?" Ben asked. "What does it mean?"

"Maybe there's a clue in the roadside-attractions guide," Maya said.

Back in the bus, Dusty was reading *RV Enthusiast* magazine. As Maya hurriedly began to explain her and Ben's sticky encounter in the V.I.L.E. trap, Ben leafed through the guidebook.

"I think I found something on the squirrel," Ben said. "According to this, white squirrels are extremely rare, but three cities in the U.S. claim to have some: Kenton, Tennessee; Marionville, Missouri; and Olney, Illinois."

"We can't go driving to all of those places," Maya said.

Dusty pulled a piece of paper out of her pocket. "We might not have to," she said. "This came over the fax while you two were out being frog bait. It's from Tina Tolltaker." She read it aloud: " 'Red van seen on Arkansas highway. Biography of Samuel Clemens spotted on dashboard.' "

Ben frowned. "How does that help us? We already know Carmen's agent is in Arkansas."

"I think I know," Maya said. "Samuel Clemens

is the real name of the author Mark Twain. He wrote *The Adventures of Huckleberry Finn*."

"That's right," Dusty said. "He lived in and wrote about—"

"Missouri!" Maya and Ben said at once.

"Right again," Dusty said.

Maya and Ben high-fived each other. "Next stop, Marionville, Missouri!" Maya cried.

6
Marionville, Missouri

"**N**ot so fast," Dusty said. "We're not going anywhere."

"What do you mean?" Ben cried. "We've got to catch up with Carmen's agent."

Maya nodded. "Besides, I think Marionville's only a couple of hours away from here. Missouri is just north of Arkansas. Marionville is in southwest Missouri, near the Arkansas border. It's part of the Ozark region, just like Eureka Springs."

"You're right about that," Dusty said. "But hear me out. First of all, Marionville is a small town with a crackerjack police force. I don't think Carmen's agent would risk wandering around there in the middle of the night. And second, I haven't had too much sleep these last two days, and neither has our friend. My guess is that he or she is sleeping like a baby somewhere, dreaming of you two up to your ankles in flypaper."

"You're probably right," Maya said. "Everyone needs to sleep."

Dusty smiled. "You can say that again. We can make camp at Beaver Lake. It's just a few minutes away. And besides," she said, "I can't let you two go running around without any shoes on."

Maya and Ben stared down at their socks, which were covered with dirt.

Ben sighed. "I guess you're right. I just hope we don't lose the trail."

The next morning the bus was back on the road bright and early.

"Next stop, shoes!" Dusty yelled from the front seat.

"And then breakfast!" Maya said. "I'm starved."

Ben got up from his seat and stretched. "No way! First we nail Carmen's agent, then we eat. We're so close. I've got a feeling we'll do it this time. Besides, there's some cold cereal in the kitchen."

Maya sighed. "I know, but I dreamed all night

about eggs and hash browns and grits. . . ."

Dusty laughed. "You're making my mouth water."

Ben ignored them. "Can't you go any faster, Dusty? The agent's probably halfway to California by now."

Dusty caught Ben's gaze in the rearview mirror. "You leave the driving to me, man. We're taking a shortcut to Marionville—the Ozark Mountain Parkway. We'll be there any minute."

A few minutes later Ben spotted a sign out the window.

" 'Welcome to Marionville, Missouri, Home of the Famous White Squirrels,' " Ben read. "We're here!"

"I'll see if we can park this baby downtown," Dusty said. "I'll go out and get you some new sneaks, and then we can start looking around." Maya and Ben told her their sizes.

"Make sure they're cool," said Maya.

"I like high-tops," said Ben.

Maya and Ben stared out the bus windows, waiting for Dusty to return.

"Marionville is a really pretty town," Maya remarked, looking at the houses, green trees, and flowers on the street before them.

"I guess." Ben sighed. "I'm too busy thinking about this case. I mean, we've come so far, and we hardly know anything about Carmen's agent. We don't even know if it's a man or a woman."

Maya put her hand on Ben's shoulder. "Don't worry. At least we've narrowed it down to four suspects. And I bet your feeling last night was right. Something's bound to happen."

"Sneakers, anyone?" Dusty shouted as she burst through the bus door.

She pulled two pairs out of a plastic bag—a small purple pair, and a larger green pair.

Ben grimaced. "Did you find a clown supply store somewhere in town?"

Dusty tossed the green pair to him. "Lace up, little man. These are the only sneakers I could find. Besides, Carmen's agent won't be looking at your feet when we nab him—or her. Let's go!"

The three stepped out of the bus into a bright, sunny morning.

"Let's head for that park across the street," Maya said, pointing. "There are a lot of trees there. That would be a good place for a stranger to hide."

"Good thinking," Ben said.

The park looked like a typical city park, with

dirt paths, benches, and playground equipment. A few mothers were out, pushing baby strollers. Two gray-haired men sat on a park bench, tossing peanuts on the ground.

Maya frowned. "Unless the agent is wearing a disguise, it doesn't look like he or she is here."

"Maybe not," Ben said. "But I see something else that's pretty cool. Look!"

Ben pointed at the feet of the two men. Three squirrels were darting around on the ground, grabbing peanuts. They were as white as snow.

"Cool!" Maya cried. "I can't believe it."

Dusty nodded. "That is quite a sight."

"Help!" A loud voice broke the early-morning quiet.

Maya turned. A blond woman in a blue jumpsuit came running up to them. She carried a large wire cage. A name tag on her shirt read SALLY STOKES. MARIONVILLE PARKS DEPARTMENT.

"What's wrong?" Maya asked.

Sally Stokes stopped. "There's been a gray squirrel sighted!"

Ben frowned. "Yeah? So what?"

"So what?" Sally said angrily. "We can't have gray squirrels in this town. Marionville is famous for its *white* squirrels. When a gray squirrel makes its way here, we trap it and send it to some other town that doesn't mind plain old gray squirrels. *That's* what!"

"Er—sorry, I guess," Ben said.

"Hey!" Maya interrupted. A gray squirrel darted right in front of her. "There it goes!"

"Good work, kid!" Sally cried. "Come on and give me a hand. We can head it off at the seesaw."

Maya, Ben, and Dusty took off like players on a football team, each heading in a different direction. The gray squirrel, frightened, ran around in circles.

Ben laughed as the squirrel headed right toward him. "I'll send him back your way, Sally!" he called out. "Get that trap ready!"

"Will do!" Sally cried.

Ben lunged at the squirrel. It turned around and headed straight back—right into Sally's trap.

"Bingo!" Sally said, holding up the trap. "We got you, you little gray guy."

"Um, Sally," Maya said, tugging on her sleeve. "I think there might be a problem. I don't think that's a gray squirrel."

Sally frowned. "What are you talking about? Nobody knows squirrels better than me." She peered into the cage.

"See that white spot on the squirrel's back?" Maya asked.

Sally leaned forward to take a closer look. "What do you know! Someone rolled him in the dust so he would look gray!"

"I bet if you gave this guy a bath, you'd find he's white all over," Maya said.

"Why would somebody go around dusting squirrels?" Dusty asked.

Ben slapped his hand to his forehead. "Oh, no! We've been tricked again! The agent must have been trying to distract us. I can't—"

The sound of squealing brakes interrupted him. They turned in the direction of the sound to see a red van speeding around a corner.

"To the bus!" Maya cried. "Sorry, Sally. We've got to run."

Dusty reached the bus first and unlocked the door. She turned the ignition key and stepped on the gas pedal.

Nothing happened.

"Keep trying, Dusty!" Ben cried.

Dusty tried again. Nothing.

"Sorry, dude," Dusty said. "I've got to check under the hood." She stepped outside.

"You were right, Ben," Maya said. "The agent

planted the fake gray squirrel to keep us busy."

Ben slammed his fist down on a chair. "I can't believe it! We've been fooled, and we don't have a single clue. The agent could be anywhere."

Dusty came back inside the bus, her hands covered with grease.

"It looks like our friend's been messing around with the bus," Dusty said. "I can fix it, but it'll take about an hour. Why don't you two go and have that breakfast Maya was dreaming about."

Maya tried to smile. "Thanks, Dusty. Maybe we'll find some clues while we're at it."

"Good idea," Ben said. "I'll bring the Ultra-Secret Sender along."

Soon Maya and Ben were sitting at a counter in a small diner, gobbling down plates of steaming scrambled eggs and crispy hash brown potatoes.

"What we need to do," Maya said between mouthfuls of food, "is ask around and see if anybody's seen a strange-looking person wearing a long dark coat, dark glasses, and a hat."

Ben took a gulp of orange juice. "This is a small town. Somebody must have seen something."

An older man sitting two stools down turned and looked at them. "Excuse me, but did y'all say dark coat and glasses?"

"Yes," Maya said excitedly. "Why, did you see someone dressed like that?"

The man nodded. "Sure did. I own the hardware store just down the street. Had a package delivered yesterday. Instructions said that an A. Vile would be in to pick it up in the morning."

"A. Vile—that must be a code name for a V.I.L.E. agent!" Maya whispered to Ben.

"What happened?" Ben asked.

The man shrugged. "Seemed kind of strange to me, but I didn't think much of it. Then sure enough, somebody walks in this morning and says they're A. Vile. Opens up the package, and it's a ball of twine. Strangest thing," the man said, scratching his head.

"Did you see what A. Vile looked like?" Maya asked.

The man shook his head. "Nope. Couldn't even tell if it was a man or a woman."

Ben was flipping through the book of roadside attractions. "Ball of twine . . . ball of twine," he muttered. "Here's something! Two cities in the U.S. have been fighting over who has the largest ball of twine: Darwin, Minnesota, and Cawker City, Kansas."

"That narrows it down," Maya said. "Maybe if we ask around we can find another clue."

Just then the Ultra-Secret Sender began to whir.

A sheet of paper shot out from the fax printer.

Ben grabbed the paper. "It's from Tina Tolltaker," he said.

Maya shook her head. "She sure has great timing, doesn't she?"

"'Red van spotted at tollbooth on Interstate Thirty-five north. Mozart blasting through window,'" Ben read.

Maya grabbed the Sender and started typing. "I've called up a highway map. It looks like I-Thirty-five goes right to Minnesota!"

"Excellent!" Ben said. "It's time to leave Mark Twain country, and head for Big Twine country!"

I just got a dispatch from my agent. This might just be my cleverest agent yet. Those tricky traps should keep those traveling gumshoes from recovering Interstate Eighty. They have only four days left . . . and The Chief will be forced to join me at V.I.L.E.!

7
Darwin, Minnesota

As Maya and Ben approached the bus, Dusty was just finishing up the repairs.

"Hey, guys!" Dusty called. "Figure out our next stop yet?"

"Darwin, Minnesota," Ben answered.

"Know it well," Dusty said. "Stopped there once when The Strolling Gnomes were playing a gig in Minneapolis. Small place, but definitely cool." Dusty began humming a tune.

"Darwin, Minnesota?" Maya said, scratching her head.

"What's the matter?" Ben asked. "Never heard of it?"

"I just can't seem to place it," Maya said. She opened up the map and spread it on the table.

Ben grinned. *Well,* he thought to himself, *Maya doesn't know* everything.

"Here it is," Maya announced. "Darwin, Minnesota, population 252."

Ben whistled. "Talk about a small town!"

Maya nodded. "That's for sure. But Darwin's only about an hour's drive from Minneapolis. And that's a big city!"

Ben sat down next to Maya and looked at the map. It looked like if they took U.S. Highway Twelve from Minneapolis and drove west, they'd hit Darwin.

"Hey, Maya, didn't we go to Minneapolis once on a case?"

"Yeah," said Maya. "We went to the Winter Carnival, trying to track down Liza Lotsa when she stole the colors from the Painted Desert."

"You two have been everywhere," said Dusty. Ben nodded.

"Minneapolis and St. Paul are known as the Twin Cities," Maya continued, typing some information into the Ultra-Secret Sender. After a few minutes a long white piece of paper came out of the Sender. "Here it is," Maya said. "Everything you ever wanted to know about the Twin Cities—and more."

Ben laughed and put his feet up on the table. "Go ahead, I'm listening."

" 'Both St. Paul and Minneapolis are on the Mississippi River,' " Maya began. " 'In fact, the Mississippi separates the two cities.

" 'Minneapolis's history began in the St. Croix River town of Stillwater, which is a short drive from the Twin Cities. And St. Paul began as a French village, known as Pig's Eye Landing,' " Maya continued.

"Pig's *what*?" Ben said.

"Pig's Eye," Maya said. " 'The village was named for Pierre "Pig's Eye" Parrant, a retired fur trader who owned a saloon in the area.' "

"So why is the city called St. Paul now instead of Pig's Eye?" Ben wanted to know.

"Probably because no one would want to live there!" Maya said with a laugh. She scanned the printout. "Here it is," she said. " 'In 1841, a Father Lucien Galtier arrived in Pig's Eye and built a chapel dedicated to St. Paul, and he asked that the city's name be changed.' "

"Hey, I wonder how long it'll take us to get to Pig's Eye," Ben interrupted.

"That's St. Paul," Maya reminded him. "But remember, we're not stopping there. We're going straight to Darwin. In fact," Maya said, looking at the road map, "we're not going to see St. Paul at all. Once we reach Minneapolis, we're going to take U.S. Highway Twelve west to Darwin. Isn't that right, Dusty?"

"Good navigating, little lady," Dusty called. "We should be there in about ten hours. Eleven, if we need to stop."

"*Eleven* hours?" Ben groaned. "In that case, I'm going to take a nap."

"A nap?" Maya said. "It's still morning!"

"I'll take my rest when I can get it," Ben said, and he headed off to his bunk.

Ben woke up to the sound of classical music blasting. "Do you mind?" Ben said as he stumbled out of his bunk. "How do you expect me to sleep with all that noise?"

"Hey, man," Dusty said. "*Never* call Beethoven noise!"

"Sorry," Ben said. "It's just that I'm really beat, and I want to sleep a little bit more."

Maya started to laugh. "Hey, sleepyhead. Take a look at your watch."

Ben looked at his watch and rubbed his eyes. "My watch must be broken," he said.

"It's not broken," Maya said with a smirk.

"You've been sleeping for *five* hours! It's about time you woke up."

Ben blushed. "You're kidding! I guess I really was tired. And now I'm hungry. I think I'll make a sandwich. Do you guys want one too?" he asked.

"Okay," said Dusty.

"Sure," Maya said. "I'll be sitting up here with Dusty. She's giving me a crash course on Beethoven. I've never met anyone so into classical music before!"

Maya called out a little while later, "Hey, Ben, what's taking so long? I'm starving!"

When Ben didn't answer, she headed back toward the kitchen. But instead of making sandwiches, Ben was busy typing some information into the Ultra-Secret Sender.

"What happened to lunch?" Maya asked.

"All that talk about classical music made me remember something," Ben said. "Our last fax from Tina told us that a red van was spotted on Interstate Thirty-five with Mozart blasting through the window."

"So?" Maya said.

"So Mozart is one of those classical guys, like Beethoven. And when I looked up our list of suspects, I discovered that Ray Zarumpus and Rhett

70

Barron don't listen to classical music. Ray likes salsa and Rhett likes rock. So that leaves us with Hammond Swiss and Polly Graph."

"Ben, you're brilliant!" Maya said, patting him on the back. "Just for that, *I'll* make the sandwiches!"

It was late at night when the bus finally rolled into Darwin. The town was quiet, and only a few houses still had lights shining through their windows.

"There it is!" Ben said, pointing to a big Plexiglas structure. He and Maya ran out of the bus. "The world's largest ball of twine. It weighs 21,140 pounds and is twelve feet in circumference."

"Who would ever have made such a thing?" Maya wanted to know.

"A man named Francis A. Johnson," Ben answered.

"Hey! What was that?" Maya shouted.

"What?" Ben asked.

"I saw a flash of light," Maya said. "It came from behind the building. Come on, let's check it out!"

Maya and Ben ran over to the Plexiglas

structure that housed the ball of twine. "I don't see anything," Ben said. "Maybe . . ."

Suddenly the light flashed again. And again. And again!

"Where's it coming from?" Maya asked, running around the building.

"Hey, Maya!" Ben called out. "Look at this."

Maya ran over to where Ben was standing. His nose was pressed up against the Plexiglas. The huge ball of twine was lit up by what seemed like a hundred little spotlights. "Pretty impressive, huh?" Ben said. "But I'm still not sure that solves our light mystery—"

Before Ben could finish his sentence, a loud sound cut through the night air. *Whoosh!* A huge piece of rope shot out of somewhere and started to wrap around their bodies. They were being tied to the building!

"The ball of twine is unraveling!" Ben cried, struggling to move.

"No, it's not," Maya said. "It's still inside. A different rope is being used to tie us up. Ben, we've fallen into another trap!"

As quickly as it had all started, it stopped. "Help!" Ben cried out. "Somebody cut us loose!"

"Dusty!" Maya called. "Come help us!"

They yelled for a while, but no one came to help them.

"It's no use," said Maya. "No one can hear us."

"Well, what do you want us to do? Just wait here? And stop wriggling around!" Ben shouted. "Every time you move, it makes the rope tighter, and I can hardly breathe," he panted.

"The reason I'm wriggling," Maya said, "is because I'm trying to get my pocketknife out of my backpack. And if I can do that, I can cut us loose."

"Oh," Ben said. "Need any help?"

"Yes," Maya said. "Once I pull it out, I'm going to hand it to you. Then I think I can open it up and get the blade out."

Maya's plan worked perfectly, and they were soon cut free.

"That was a close one," Ben said, rubbing his arms. "Good thing you were wearing that backpack. Otherwise I don't know how we would have gotten out. I wonder why Dusty didn't hear us."

Maya and Ben ran back to the bus. There was Dusty, sitting at the steering wheel, hands, feet, and mouth bound.

"Oh, no, Dusty!" Maya cried. "Are you all right?"

Dusty nodded.

Maya pulled out her pocketknife and quickly cut Dusty free.

"What happened?" Ben wanted to know.

"Someone wearing a long coat and dark glasses came onto the bus and bopped me on the head. When I came to, I was all tied up. Tried to yell, but it was no use. I figured you two would return eventually," Dusty said.

"We got tied up too!" Maya said. "So are you okay?"

"I've been better," Dusty replied. "Especially my head!"

Just then Maya spotted something. "Wait a second, look at this!" She bent down under the dashboard and pulled out a large, dried cob of corn.

"Yo!" Dusty exclaimed. "That was probably what that dude—or dudette—bopped me with!"

"This has to be some sort of clue," Maya said. "Our V.I.L.E. agent is getting sloppy!"

Ben pulled out the roadside-attractions guide and flipped through it. "Corn husk. Corncob," he said. "I found it! There's a place called the Mitchell Corn Palace in Mitchell, South Dakota. That has to be where our henchperson is headed next!"

"You're right!" Maya said. "Come on, let's hit the road."

Dusty just rubbed her head and stared at Maya and Ben. "Sorry, guys. But I'm not going anywhere. Not now, at least."

"Dusty's right," Ben said. "She just drove about eleven hours straight, and got knocked on the head," he reminded Maya. "She's exhausted."

"You're right," Maya agreed. "Let's hit our bunks, and all get some rest. Besides, the henchperson probably thinks we'll be *tied up* for a while!"

8
Mitchell, South Dakota

Maya and Ben woke up early the next morning to the sound of the fax machine whirring. Maya ran over to the machine and pulled out the printout. It was from Tina Tolltaker: "Red van spotted driving west on Interstate Ninety."

"Interstate Ninety!" Maya cried out, running to the map. "That means Carmen's agent is at least one hundred miles ahead of us. Quick, Dusty, Ben, get up. We've got to get out of here!"

Dusty shook her head. "No need to worry, my little gumshoe. If that agent takes I-Ninety, he or she will be stuck in terrible traffic. Because I-Eighty is gone, people are flocking to all the other roadways. We'll take the back roads and catch up in no time."

Soon they were on the road again, driving on "blue highways" and back roads. Dusty sure knew her way around.

"I can't stand these long drives!" Maya exclaimed, pacing back and forth. "Maybe we should contact The Chief and get a faster means of transportation, like a helicopter or a plane."

"If we were in the air, we could miss some valuable clues," Ben said. "But speaking of The Chief, maybe we should check in with her and give her an update."

Maya nodded. "Good idea." She opened up the Ultra-Secret Sender, and a few minutes later The Chief's image appeared on the screen. She was sitting at her desk, her head in her hands.

"Chief!" Maya cried out, worried. It was not like The Chief to act like this—she was usually so together.

"Gumshoes," The Chief responded. "Have you anything to report?"

Maya and Ben gave her an update. But The Chief did not look hopeful.

"The country is a mess," The Chief reported. "The airports are in a state of chaos. The major roadways are all having the biggest backups in history. There are abandoned cars everywhere. And some people are actually scared to drive—they're afraid that all the major highways will disappear. In fact, there has been a series of such threats called in to local authorities."

"Do you think Carmen is behind the threats?" Ben asked.

The Chief shook her head. "No. Carmen is just after me. And I'm sure she's enjoying this little game she's playing. I think the other threats are just copycats calling in. I don't think we need to take them seriously."

Maya breathed a sigh of relief. "Don't worry, Chief," she said. "We're on the right trail. We'll recover I-Eighty, and nab Carmen, too."

"Well, let's hope so," The Chief said. "You have only four days left, counting today. After that— well, I don't want to think about it."

Maya looked over at Ben. He looked worried. She felt the same way too. But she knew that feeling that way would only make matters worse. They needed to have a positive attitude. Maya drew in a deep breath and smiled. "We'll check in again, Chief," she said. "And don't worry—we have everything under control."

"Wow," Ben said after they had put the Sender away. "I guess I was so caught up in tracking down

Carmen's agent, I forgot about the actual crime and all the chaos it's causing."

"Me too." Maya nodded.

"Between the abandoned cars and the traffic jams, important supplies like food probably aren't getting delivered," Ben said. "This really *is* a national emergency!" he shouted.

"Calm down, Ben," Maya said. "Remember, we have to remain levelheaded."

"You're right, Maya," Ben said.

"Now, let's get some information about our next stop, the Corn Palace," Maya suggested. "I want to be as informed as possible. That way, maybe we won't fall into any traps."

She got a printout on the Corn Palace from the Sender. " 'The Corn Palace is located in Mitchell, South Dakota. Mitchell, situated in the James River valley, is one of the larger cities of South Dakota. It receives between eighteen and twenty-six inches of annual rainfall, which sustains tall grasses and excellent crops of corn and other grains. In fact, Mitchell calls itself the Corn Capital of the World. Its high-school teams are the Kernels, and its radio station call letters are K-O-R-N—' "

"How *corny*," Ben interrupted.

"Very funny," Maya said. " 'The Corn Palace,

79

built in 1892, is a crazy combination of minarets, turrets, and kiosks,'" she continued. "'It stands five stories high, covers a square block, and is built out of—'"

"Wait," Ben interrupted. "Let me guess. *Corn*crete!"

Maya rolled her eyes. "Wrong. *Con*crete. 'But the outside of the building is completely covered with murals made of native South Dakota corn, grain, and grass. Ears of corn are sawed length-wise and then nailed flat to outside panels that are changed every year.'"

"Gosh," Ben said. "I wonder if they string pop-corn on the building at Christmastime."

"It wouldn't surprise me," Maya said.

"All this talk about corn is making me a little hungry," Ben announced. "How about I fix us a snack. Say, corn dogs and corn chips? Just to get us in the mood."

Maya laughed. "Sure!"

After a long ride, the bus finally pulled up in front of the Mitchell Corn Palace.

"If I didn't know better, I would swear we were in Russia," Maya said, looking up at the building. "This place looks like a corn version of the Kremlin!"

"You know, you're right," Ben said. "Maybe this place's nickname is the *Korn*lin!"

Maya groaned. "That was a bad one, Ben."

"Well, let's stop standing around cracking jokes," Ben said, annoyed that Maya didn't like his pun. He thought it was pretty good, himself. "Carmen's agent has a couple of hours on us. For all we know, he or she has come and gone already."

"Maybe, maybe not," Maya replied. "Like Dusty said, the agent could have been caught in traffic on I-Ninety. The agent might have just arrived too."

They stepped inside.

"Hey, look at that," she said, pointing to a huge popcorn machine.

"I've never seen anything like this before," Ben said, walking over to the machine. It was about six feet tall.

"It looks like a giant air popper," he said. "Let's see if it works."

Before Maya could object, Ben pressed the on switch and the machine buzzed to life. And before Maya could pull Ben out of the way, popcorn started pouring out of the machine. Not just a little popcorn—a *ton* of popcorn.

"Help!" Ben cried. "Get this stuff off me!" Popcorn rained down on his head. They were being buried in popcorn! "We've got to turn off the machine!" he shouted.

Maya tried the off switch, but nothing happened. "I think it's stuck," she said.

A crowd had gathered around Maya and Ben. "Look at that, Mom," Maya heard a little girl say. "It's a popcorn party!"

"This must be a new sideshow at the Corn Palace," Ben heard someone else say.

"This is not a party! Or a sideshow!" Maya cried. "We've got to stop this popcorn popper and get out of here!" But Maya and Ben could not move. They were covered in a mountain of popcorn!

Suddenly, through the crowd, Maya spotted a figure wearing dark glasses, a long coat, and a hat. And the figure was headed out the door.

"Carmen's agent!" Maya shouted. "Quick, Ben. Think of something. We've got to get out of here!"

"Start eating!" Ben said. He grabbed a handful of popcorn and shoved it in his mouth.

"Come join the popcorn party!" Maya shouted to the crowd. "All the popcorn you can eat!"

Before long, Maya and Ben were freed from

the popcorn trap. "This way!" Maya shouted, pointing to the exit.

When they got outside, they saw Carmen's agent leaning against the red van, eating something out of a huge box.

"I wonder why the agent is just standing there," Ben said.

"Because he or she probably thinks we've been buried by popcorn, so there's no need to rush," Maya explained.

"Well, he or she is in for a surprise," Ben said. "V.I.L.E. agent!" Ben shouted. "You're under arrest."

Startled, the agent dropped the box and jumped into the van. The contents of the box spilled all over the ground.

"Stop!" Maya cried, running toward the agent. "You're un—" She slipped and fell on the hard asphalt.

"Maya, are you all ri—" Ben slipped too and landed right next to Maya. Before they had a chance to get up, the van pulled away.

"Missed him!" Maya cried.

"Or her!" Ben added.

"Hey, what is this stuff?" Maya asked, picking up what they had slipped on. "Candy-coated popcorn. Peanuts."

"Cracker Jack!" Ben cried. "The agent must have picked up the box here—I bet it has a clue from Carmen inside."

Maya walked over to the Cracker Jack box the agent had dropped. "This is some huge box," she commented. "I don't think I've ever seen one so big before."

"What about the prize?" Ben asked.

"The prize?" Maya said.

"You know, candy-coated popcorn, peanuts, and a prize," Ben said.

"Oh, right," Maya said. She reached inside the box. But instead of finding one prize, she found several: a purple plastic spaceship, three purple plastic aliens, and one purple plastic ray gun.

"I wonder what that's all about," Ben said.

"Hmm . . ." Maya said. "Come on, let's get back to the bus and figure out this mystery."

Once inside, Maya flipped through the road-side-attractions book.

"What are you looking for?" Dusty asked.

"UFOs, or any weird attraction with aliens and spaceships," Maya replied. She sighed, and put down the book. "The book is full of places like that! I don't know where to start."

Dusty looked thoughtful. "You know, when I

was driving the bus for the Far-Out Spacemen, they always made me stop in Roswell, New Mexico. They say aliens landed there years ago."

Ben frowned. "It sounds good, but what if we're wrong?"

"I know!" Maya cried. "Dusty, what road takes us to New Mexico?"

"From here we'll head west on the back roads and hit I-Twenty-five in Wyoming. Then we'll take it south all the way to New Mexico," Dusty said.

Maya ran to the Ultra-Secret Sender. "Let's fax Tina Tolltaker and ask her to alert her friends on I-Twenty-five. If the van isn't spotted soon, we can change course."

"Maya," Ben said. "You're out of this world!"

Maya was feeling generous. So this time she laughed at his joke.

9
Roswell, New Mexico

Moonlight shone through the bus windows as the gumshoes sped south on Interstate Twenty-five.

Ben was staring at the Ultra-Secret Sender, his chin in his hands. "It's been an hour since Tina Tolltaker last faxed us," he said. "Maybe Carmen's agent left the highway."

Dusty shook her head. "Doesn't seem likely, dude. Your evil friend wouldn't have traveled this far on Twenty-five unless he or she was heading to New Mexico."

"Where are we, anyway?" Maya asked, yawning.

"Colorado, just north of Denver," Dusty replied. "Not a bad place for a rest stop. I'll wager that's why nobody's spotted the red van for a while."

Maya yawned again. "Sounds good to me."

Ben sighed. "I guess so. But promise me we'll wake up *really* early."

"Cross my heart, dude," Dusty said, leaning back in the front seat. "Sweet dreams, everybody."

The whirring of the Ultra-Secret Sender woke Ben out of a sound sleep. He leaped to his feet.

"Wake up, you two!" he cried. "It's from Tina Tolltaker. The van was just spotted in Colorado Springs heading south on Twenty-five."

Maya groaned and pulled her pillow over her face. "Doesn't anyone in V.I.L.E. ever sleep? The sun's not even up yet."

"I can see it peeking over the horizon," Dusty said, looking out the driver's side window. "Colorado Springs isn't that far away. We can catch up if we burn rubber." She pulled her chair upright, adjusted her bandanna, and started the engine with a roar.

In the bus's kitchen, Maya and Ben fixed glasses of orange juice and bowls of cold cereal.

"How far are we from Roswell?" Ben called to Dusty.

"It's quite a ways yet," Dusty replied. "That

sun'll be down again before we get there."

Ben sighed. "What are we going to do all day?"

Maya picked up the roadside-attractions guide. "I'd like to know more about Roswell," she said, turning the pages. "It's a pretty fascinating story."

"What happened?" Ben asked.

Maya looked at the book. "It says here that in 1947, a farmer found the remains of some kind of crash in his field outside Roswell. The material was really weird—some strange kind of metal. So he took it into town, and some guys at the air force base outside of Roswell got ahold of it."

"What was it?" Ben asked.

"That's where it gets complicated," Maya said. "A military officer told the press that it was a flying disc—a UFO. But the next day, the military changed its story. They said it was just a downed weather balloon."

Ben shrugged. "So what's the big deal?"

"The story didn't end there," Maya said. "Years later, many people who lived in Roswell at the time came forward and said they saw the wrecked UFO. Some people even say they saw the bodies of dead aliens in the wreck! But they were afraid to talk about it."

Ben shook his head. "People don't *really*

believe in aliens, do they?"

"Those guys in the Far-Out Spacemen believed every word of it," Dusty called back. "They loved to go to Roswell, in hopes that the aliens would come back down from the sky."

"See what I mean!" Ben said. He laughed. "Great. Not only do we have to worry about V.I.L.E., but now we have to worry about little green men from outer space!"

The sun was high in the sky when Dusty finally called out, "We're getting closer, dudes. We made it to New Mexico!"

Maya and Ben walked up to the front of the bus. "New Mexico? We're still in the United States, right?" Ben asked.

"Yep." Dusty nodded.

"A lot of people think New Mexico is part of Mexico," Maya chimed in. "But it's one of the fifty states."

"I knew that," Ben said, blushing.

"In fact," Maya continued, "it touches five other states in the U.S. In the northwest corner, Utah, Colorado, Arizona, and New Mexico all meet. That spot is called the Four Corners."

"Is Roswell near the Four Corners?" Ben asked.

"Nope," Dusty said. "Roswell's in the southeastern part of the state. Once we get to the state capital, we'll get off Twenty-five and take U.S. Highway 285 south right into Roswell."

"The state capital?" Maya asked. "That's Santa Fe, right?"

Dusty smiled. "Right on, man."

Ben was fanning his face with a road map. "Can't you put on the air-conditioning? It's really hot in here."

"Open the windows, dude," Dusty said. "New Mexico is a hot, dry state."

"You can say that again," Maya said. "Roswell is in New Mexico's plains region. It's miles and miles of flat, treeless land, with a few small, rolling hills here and there."

"The perfect landing spot for aliens," Dusty said in a spooky voice.

"Cut it out!" Ben said, rolling his eyes.

A few hours and a couple of rest stops later, Dusty called Maya and Ben to the front of the bus.

"We're almost in Roswell," Dusty said. "Do you have any idea where to find the V.I.L.E. agent?"

"I thought about that," Maya said. "The roadside

91

guidebook lists two UFO attractions: the International UFO Museum and Research Center, and the UFO Enigma Museum. I wonder what an Enigma is."

"It's a mystery or a riddle," Ben said. He shrugged. "I had it on a vocabulary test."

"Your teacher sure is crazy about vocabulary tests," Maya said. She looked thoughtful. "A riddle, huh? Maybe we should try there first. This V.I.L.E. agent sure seems to like riddles and tricks."

"Good idea!" Dusty chimed in. She took the guidebook from Maya. "According to this, the museum is next to the air force base. We'll be there in a few minutes."

Maya and Ben stared out the front window. Land stretched out before them as far as they could see. Every once in a while a cactus or a cluster of houses dotted the landscape.

"Looks like we're here," Dusty said as they pulled up in front of a small, square building. A sign over the door read UFO ENIGMA MUSEUM. She parked the bus and opened the front door.

Maya and Ben stepped out into the hot night. The museum was on a street with a few other businesses. In the distance they could see the gates and military barracks of the air force base.

The small street was crowded with people. Most were dressed in shorts or jeans. Some wore plastic space helmets and antennae.

"What's going on?" Ben wondered aloud.

"They're coming!" a teenager with an alien face on his T-shirt told Ben. "The aliens are coming tonight!"

Ben shook his head. "Get a grip. Come on, Maya, let's check out the museum."

"I'm coming too," Dusty said. "I dig this alien stuff."

Maya hurried behind Ben and paid her admission. "Just because someone believes in aliens doesn't mean they're crazy," she hissed. "Anything's possible, right?"

"Whatever," Ben said, walking into the main exhibit room. "If you want to— What's this?"

Maya and Ben stopped short. In front of them was a lit display of a UFO crash site. A silver, saucer-shaped spaceship with a red light on top sat in the middle of a fake dirt field. The bodies of aliens with large bald heads and giant eyes were lying next to the saucer.

"They look just like real aliens," Maya whispered.

"It's *so* fake," Ben said, rolling his eyes.

The sound of loud voices spilled into the quiet room.

"They're here! They're here at last!"

Ben sped out of the museum, and Maya and Dusty followed right behind him. Outside, a crowd of people was pointing in the air.

A saucer-shaped object was floating in the sky. It had red and green lights that were blinking like crazy.

"It's a UFO!" Ben screamed. He turned and ran for the bus. "Let's get out of here!"

Dusty reached out and grabbed Ben's shirt. "Chill out, dude. I've never heard of a UFO with a string attached to it before."

"A string?" Ben said sheepishly.

Dusty pointed. A piece of white string stretched from the top of the saucer to a nearby tree.

"Oh, no!" Ben groaned. "Another trick!"

The crowd began to talk in hushed whispers as Maya ran to the tree.

"It's going to beam her up!" someone screamed.

Maya shinnied up the tree and cut the string with her pocketknife. The saucer fell to the ground with a thud.

The crowd let out a collective groan. They were

very disappointed it was just a fake.

Ben ran over and picked up the "UFO." "It's just two pie plates," he called out. "They're painted to look like a UFO, and there's battery-operated Christmas lights wrapped around them. I, uh, I knew all along that it was a fake."

"Sure you did," Maya said teasingly. "But that doesn't matter. We've been tricked again! We'll never find the V.I.L.E. henchperson now."

The sound of a loud car horn pierced the night air.

The gumshoes turned. A van was trying to make its way down the street, but the street was crowded with UFO seekers.

"It's the red van!" Maya cried. "It hasn't gotten away yet!"

Dusty reached the bus first, and Maya and Ben followed her inside. The crowd was thinning, and Dusty pulled the bus right behind the van.

"It's going off the main road!" Dusty cried. "Heading into the plains! Hold on to your hats, dudes!"

The bus screeched as Dusty followed the van over the dry, flat ground. Soon the bus and the van were side by side.

Maya and Ben leaned out of an open window.

They could see the van's driver.

"I can't see a face!" Maya called out.

"Neither can I!" Ben cried. He cupped his hands over his mouth. "Stop, in the name of ACME!"

Suddenly the bus began to cough and choke.

"We're running out of gas!" Dusty yelled.

"Nooo!" Maya and Ben cried, and the bus ground to a halt. They watched the red van disappear into the darkness.

"This can't be happening!" Maya said. "We're out of gas. We're out of clues. And we're almost out of time!"

The latest report from my agent is promising. Those gumshoes are stranded in the middle of nowhere—I love it! Soon I'll have Interstate Eighty in my hands—and The Chief at my side!

10
Texas Canyon, Arizona

"**T**his isn't good, gumshoes," The Chief said. Maya and Ben had just finished explaining their latest problem. Even on the small video screen of the Ultra-Secret Sender, Maya and Ben could tell that The Chief looked extremely unhappy.

"We were so close!" Ben said.

"Not close enough," The Chief snapped. "I'm sending one of our informants in the area to help you out of this mess. He should be there by sunrise. In the meantime, I'd suggest that you try to figure out how to get back on the henchperson's trail."

"Yes, Chief," Maya and Ben said meekly.

The screen went blank.

"What will we do now?" Maya wailed. "We don't have anything to go on."

Ben picked up the fake flying saucer. "Maybe there's a clue here somewhere." He stared at it closely.

"Hey!" he exclaimed. "Whoever put this little baby together did a pretty nice job painting it. Wasn't there a V.I.L.E. agent who likes to paint?"

Maya started pulling up the dossiers. "Hammond Swiss!" she cried.

"I'm going to fax Wanda at ACME and see if she'll issue a warrant for him," Ben said.

Maya grabbed his arm. "Not so fast, Ben. I'm just not sure that's enough to go on. We still haven't ruled out Polly Graph. We've made mistakes before. I'd hate to make another one."

Dusty nodded. "The Chief seemed pretty ticked off already. It'd be a shame to get her riled up again."

Ben hesitated. "I . . . I don't know. It's such a good clue!"

"Let's just sleep on it, okay?" Maya said. "We might find more clues in the morning."

"Okay," Ben said reluctantly.

The sun was just rising when a loud knock on the bus door woke everyone up.

"I'll get it," Dusty said.

Maya and Ben peered over Dusty's shoulder as the door opened. A tall, thin man with a weathered face and short white hair stood there smiling. He wore a blue shirt, a bolo tie, and a brown ten-gallon hat. Behind him a large gray horse stood patiently.

"Howdy, pardners," the man said. "Name's Wild Will. The Chief sent me. Told me you were in a heap o' trouble."

Maya and Ben exchanged glances. This was the ACME informant?

Dusty pumped Will's hand. "Pleased to meet you, cowboy dude. We sure could use some help. This baby's out of gas."

Will motioned to the horse. Two red gas cans were slung over the saddle. "Old Blue's got what you need, little lady. Help yourself."

Dusty climbed out of the bus and walked toward the horse. Maya and Ben stepped out and faced Wild Will.

"I understand you two might need some help getting back on V.I.L.E.'s trail," Will said. "I'm glad to lend a hand if I can."

"Sure," Maya said. "We're kind of stumped."

"Tell me about this feller yer chasin'," Will said. "What kind of wheels is he driving?"

"The driver could be a woman," Maya pointed out. "We're not sure."

"*You're* not sure," Ben said. "To answer your question, it's a red van."

Will walked several yards in front of the bus and knelt down in the sandy dirt. "I can see the tracks pretty clearly," he called out as he walked back. "That's a start. What else do y'all know?"

Ben thought for a minute. "Well, we know the agent likes weird roadside attractions."

Dusty walked up to them, wiping her hands on her jeans. "She's all gassed up and ready to go!"

"Go where?" Ben said.

"I'll tell you what," Will said. "Why don't I get on Old Blue and follow the van's trail. Y'all can follow me. If I see something unusual, I'll stop."

"Sounds good to me," Dusty said. "Let's go!"

The bus crawled westward behind Wild Will and Old Blue for almost two hours before the cowboy came to a halt. Dusty stopped the bus.

"Did you find something?" Maya asked, squinting as she stepped out into the bright sunlight.

Will knelt on the ground. "Looks like your friend stopped here for the night and made a fire," he said. He picked up a handful of ashes, which fell through his fingers. "They're still warm. This feller's not too far ahead."

"Hear that?" Ben said. "He said 'feller'—I'm positive it's Hammond Swiss."

"That painting clue isn't enough to go on," Maya snapped. "Let's wait until we get more information before we request a warrant."

"But there's no time to lose!" Ben protested.

Wild Will cleared his throat. "If you two coyotes are done howlin' at each other, I've got something else to show ya," he said. He opened his hand and revealed a charred piece of paper. "Found this in the ashes."

Maya gently picked it up. "Most of the paper is burned, but there are a few words left: 'Ten . . . Whale . . . Texas . . .'"

"Whales in Texas?" Ben asked. He opened the guidebook. "Maybe there's an aquarium there."

Maya shook her head. "That doesn't make sense, Ben. We've been heading west for miles. Texas is east of Roswell. It just doesn't add up." She typed some info into the Sender. "I'm calling up a list of all places with Texas as part of the name."

Maya studied the screen for a minute. "Here's something. There's a place called Texas Canyon. It's off Interstate Ten in Arizona—that's west of here."

"Texas Canyon!" Wild Will exclaimed. "That's one of the purdiest places in the whole U.S. of A. There's some amazing giant rocks there. There's even one that's shaped like a whale."

"A whale!" Maya and Ben cried.

Dusty smiled. "I guess I know where we're headed." She turned and hugged the cowboy. "Thanks for the gas, dude."

Will blushed. "My pleasure, ma'am."

"And thanks for helping us get back on the trail," Maya added.

"You're welcome," Will said, climbing back on Old Blue. "Just do me a favor and catch that varmint!"

"We're about five hours away from Texas Canyon," Dusty said as Will rode off. "Why don't you cowpokes rustle us up some vittles?"

Maya giggled. "Sounds like Wild Will has rubbed off on you, Dusty."

Dusty grinned. "Yee-ha!"

Maya kept busy on the five-hour trip by reading a printout of information about Arizona.

"The Grand Canyon is in Arizona," Maya said. "Did you know it's 217 miles long?"

"Will we get to see it?" Ben asked.

"Not where we're going," Maya said. "The Grand Canyon is in northwest Arizona. Texas Canyon is in the southeast. That's real desert country."

Ben stretched and looked out the window. "That would explain all these giant cactuses. Is there anything interesting to see around here?"

Maya studied the printout. "We'll be close to Tucson, a major city, and Tombstone, which used to be a big city in the Old West. Wild Will would fit in great there. There are lots of ghost towns around there, too."

Ben groaned. "Great. First aliens, now ghosts."

"But the coolest thing we'll see is Texas Canyon," Maya continued. "It's filled with huge balancing rocks—rocks piled on top of one another. The guidebook says it looks like a giant's playground. Like some giant's kid was playing with the rocks and left them stacked on top of each other."

"Balancing rocks?" Ben asked. "I can't picture it."

"Maybe this will help," Dusty called. She pulled the bus into a rest area.

Maya and Ben looked out the front window. Huge rock formations jutted up from the ground in front of them.

"Cool," Ben said under his breath. "They *do* look like a giant's building blocks."

"Yeah," Maya said. "Now we've just got to find the rock that looks like a whale. According to this map, we've got to walk down Dragoon Road. It's just ahead."

The three got off the bus and walked down the road. Mesquite trees and more balancing rocks lined their path.

"I don't see any whales," Ben complained. "These rocks just look like a lot of blobs."

Dusty pointed ahead. "Even that one?" she asked, smiling.

Ben raised his head, his mouth open in surprise. Just off the road loomed a giant, whale-shaped rock. It was perched on a much smaller rock.

"It must be about twenty feet long," Maya said, awestruck, "and just as high. How is it balancing on that small rock? It looks like magic or something."

"It's pretty cool," Ben admitted. "But let's not get carried away. If the henchperson's been here,

I'm sure there's another trick waiting for us. We've got to keep our eyes open. Anything could hap—"

"Ben!" Maya screamed. "Look out!"

Ben looked over his shoulder. A round rock twice his size was rolling right toward him!

"Move it, dude!" Dusty screamed. "You're headed for pancake city!"

11
Gold Hill, Oregon

"**W**atch out!" Maya cried, pushing Ben out of the way.

Ben closed his eyes and rolled his body into a tight ball. Moments later the huge boulder rolled past him, spewing dirt and dust in his face.

"Ben, are you all right?" he heard Maya cry out.

"Yo, little friend," Dusty called. "Did you make it?"

It had happened so suddenly that Ben was still in a state of shock. He took a deep breath and slowly stood up.

"I'm fine, thanks to you guys," Ben said, wiping the dirt from his face. "Just a little shaken up, that's all."

Maya ran over and gave him a hug. "Well, I'm glad."

"Me too, dude," Dusty said, ruffling Ben's hair.

Ben blushed and straightened out his T-shirt. "Well, I guess our V.I.L.E. friend really meant business this time," he said. "That was really meant to *stop* us—for good." He shuddered.

"That must mean we're getting very close," Maya said. "Come on, let's head up top and see if the agent left any clues as to his or her next stop."

After searching for a while, the gumshoes had come up with nothing.

"What do we do now?" Ben asked, kicking the dirt. "We can't call up The Chief and tell her we've reached a dead end. This would be our last case, for sure. And hers too," he added. "We have to do something!"

"Yo, dudes!" Dusty called from the bus before Maya had a chance to answer. "Fax for you!"

Maya and Ben raced to the bus. The fax was from Tina Tolltaker. "'Red van just spotted in Phoenix, heading west on Interstate Ten,'" Maya read.

"Let's step on it, Dusty!" Ben shouted.

And they were off.

"So what do we do now?" Maya asked, pacing back and forth in the bus. "We don't know where we're headed. The V.I.L.E. agent could turn off at any time, and we'd be sunk!"

"Good thinking, Maya," Ben said. "I'm going to fax Tina and have her put her informants on triple double alert! This is a national emergency!"

Ben's warning must have worked, because they started to get a continuous stream of faxes informing them that the van was still on I-Ten. Then, about five hours later, they received a new tip: "'Red van spotted on Interstate Five in Los Angeles, heading north,'" Maya read.

"The agent is heading up through California!" Ben shouted.

The road seemed endless. They passed through many towns—Lebec, Caswell, Old River, Lost Hills, Three Rocks. The drive took hours and hours, and periodically Dusty had to stop for gas, or to take a quick nap. Maya and Ben took turns sleeping. But the faxes kept on coming; they were headed in the right direction.

"Hey, Maya!" Ben shouted, shaking her arm. "Wake up! I think we have a clue here!"

Maya rubbed her eyes. Why couldn't she ever get some solid sleep? She didn't even want to know what time it was. "What is it?" she asked Ben with a yawn.

"This is from a toll taker in Sacramento: 'Red van spotted. Stopped to ask directions to the Vortex,'" Ben read.

"Is that all they said, 'the vortex'?" Maya asked. She was wide awake now.

Ben nodded. He opened up the Ultra-Secret Sender and began typing. "Got it!" he said. "The Oregon Vortex, in Gold Hill, Oregon."

Maya picked up the roadside-attractions guidebook and leafed through it. "It's in here, too," she said. "There's some sort of electromagnetic force at the Vortex that causes all sorts of unexplained phenomena. Gee, this henchperson is weird. UFOs, aliens, strange balancing rocks, now this."

Ben shuddered. "Gives me the creeps," he said.

"I thought you didn't believe in this stuff," Maya said.

"Well, something about unexplained phenomena gives me the willies," Ben said.

"Must have been that fall you took," Maya said. "Anyway, it says here that the Oregon Vortex is a spherical field of force, half above ground, half below. The magnetic influence reaches high into the atmosphere, enough to be reported by pilots flying at forty thousand feet."

"I don't buy it," Ben said, shaking his head. "It's probably just some huge man-made underground device that produces the weird effects."

"Oh, yeah?" Maya said. "Like what?"

"Like . . . I don't know," Ben said, turning away.

Maya continued reading about the Vortex. "'Within the force field, light rays seem to bend, trees don't grow straight, and even people can't stand straight. Plus, no animals live there—they've all disappeared into another part of the forest, and birds fly over but do not land.' Cool, huh?"

"I'm not listening," Ben said.

"Doo-doo, doo-doo. Doo-doo, doo-doo," Maya taunted, waving her fingers in front of Ben's face.

"Cut it out, Maya!" Ben said, hiding his face.

"What's the matter, Ben?" Maya asked. "Afraid of the unknown?"

"I just think this place is going to be creepy," Ben said with a shudder. "That's all."

"Creepy?" Maya said incredulously. "I think it's going to be cool! Wake me when we get there. I'm going back to sleep."

"I'm too creeped out to sleep," Ben said. "How are you doing, Dusty?" he asked. "Need to stop for a rest?"

"Quit stalling for time, dude. I'm with Maya," Dusty said. "I can't wait to get there. This is going to be some awesome experience. Psychedelic, even!"

Ben put his hands over his ears. "I don't want to hear about it. Or think about it!" he exclaimed.

Dusty woke Maya and Ben when they were in the town of Medford. "Not much longer, now," Dusty informed them. "Soon we'll be experiencing—"

"I don't want to hear about it," Ben said, putting his hands over his ears.

Maya laughed. "Well, maybe you'd like to hear a little about Medford, just to get your mind off things."

Ben took a deep breath and nodded. "Okay. What do you know?"

"Medford is a beautiful place. Aunt Velma—I mean The Chief—took me there a couple of years ago," Maya said.

"On a case?" Ben asked.

"No," Maya said. "It was a family vacation. You know . . ."

"Oh, yeah," Ben said. He was so wrapped up in things that for a moment he had forgotten The Chief was Maya's aunt.

"Anyway," Maya continued, "Medford is in a rich agricultural area, and there are tons of farmers' markets around where you can buy fresh fruit, vegetables, and nuts."

"Sounds exciting to me," Ben said, rolling his eyes.

"Just wait," Maya said. "We didn't spend our time shopping. We spent it hiking and whitewater rafting."

"Now, that sounds more like you," Ben said.

Maya nodded. "We spent one day hiking at a place called Bear Creek. I'll never forget the air there. It was so crisp and clear. And the Douglas fir trees just shot up to the sky."

"Sounds nice," Ben said.

"Then the next day we drove a little bit north and went whitewater rafting on the Rogue River. That river had the most amazing rapids! I nearly fell out of the raft a couple of times!" Maya said with a laugh.

"I remember that, after the trip down the river, I was so starving we went to a cute little restaurant somewhere in town," she said. "I had the most delicious pear pancakes there!"

"Pear?" Ben said, crinkling his nose. "That doesn't sound very appetizing."

"Well, you'd be surprised," Maya said. "Maybe after we check out this Vortex place, we can try to find that restaurant."

"Great," Ben said. "I have so much to look forward to. A weirdo place and then weirdo pancakes."

The bus pulled to a stop. "We're here, dudes!" Dusty called out. "Mind if I join you on this one?" she asked.

"Sure thing, Dusty," Maya said. "Maybe you can keep an eye on Ben."

"Very funny," Ben said, stepping off the bus. "I bet this place is nothing more than a tourist trap."

"That's what they all say!" a voice said.

Maya and Ben turned to look. The voice belonged to a teenage boy, probably about sixteen or seventeen years old, with long brown scraggly hair tied back in a ponytail and a ring in his eyebrow. He wore a tattered leather jacket, an old flannel shirt, ripped jeans, and hiking boots.

"Do you work here?" Maya asked.

"Nope," the boy said. "I just come here to chill out sometimes. And watch all the tourists' reactions."

Dusty stepped off the bus, a camera slung over her shoulder.

"Dusty?" the boy called out. "Dusty Rhoads? Is that really you?"

Dusty stopped and looked at the boy quizzically.

"Aren't you the Dusty Rhoads who toured with the Black Holes? Don't you remember me? I'm Spade. Wherever Black Hole went, so did I," Spade said.

Dusty ran over to him. "Spade, man," she said, giving Spade her crazy handshake. "I didn't recognize you with your short hair. What's been going on?"

Short hair? Maya thought. *Spade's hair must have been* really *long before*.

"I've just been hanging around this place, mostly," Spade said. "What have you been doing, Dusty? Have you taken up baby-sitting?"

Maya stormed up to Spade and scowled at him. "We're *not* babies," she said. "We happen to be detectives, working on a very important case."

"Whoa!" Spade said. "The Vortex must be having an effect on me. I thought I just heard you say you're detectives."

"Well, we are!" Maya shouted.

"It's true," Dusty agreed.

"Whatever you say," Spade said. "Cute game," he whispered to Dusty.

"I heard that!" Maya shouted.

"Maya," Ben interrupted. "Let's not waste our

115

time with this guy. Let's check out this place and get out of here."

"Well, your first step should be that shack," Spade volunteered, pointing to a building.

"What is that place?" Ben asked. "And why is it slanted?"

"It's the House of Mystery," Spade said. "The center of the Vortex. On the ground, the spherical force occupies a circle with a diameter of 165 feet, four and a half inches," he explained. "The shack is slanted because it slid down the hill to its current position. Inside that shack all forces of nature go haywire!"

"Cool!" Dusty said. "Let's check it out!"

"You'd better let us go first," Maya said, stepping in front of Dusty and Spade. "Carmen's agent could be hiding out in there. And he or she could be dangerous."

"Yeah," said Spade with a laugh. "You'd better let our little detective friends go first. You never know what kind of danger could be lurking inside!"

Maya scowled at Spade, and then led the group inside the shack.

"I need to get some more information about this place," Ben said, pulling out the Ultra-Secret Sender.

"Wait a second!" he shouted. "The Sender's down! This is impossible—nothing like this has ever happened before!"

"I told you," Spade said. "It's the Vortex. It's—"

"Shhh!" Maya said. "Carmen's agent could be hiding in here."

Ben stepped forward cautiously. "It's not so bad," he said, turning around.

"Hey!" he shouted at Maya. "How did you get so tall?" He rubbed his eyes. Was he going crazy?

Maya turned around and looked back at Ben. "Hey, shrimp!" she said with a laugh. "You look tiny from over here!"

Just then Ben's body began to sway. "I'm not feeling so great, Maya. I'm having trouble standing up straight."

Maya rushed over to her friend. Suddenly, from out of nowhere, a pair of hands shot out and shoved her right into Ben. The two collided, and before they knew it, their world went black.

12
Klamath, California

"**A**re you dudes all right?" Dusty asked, shaking Maya and Ben.

Maya looked up. Dusty and Spade were standing over her. Ben was lying on the ground close by.

Maya slammed her fist into the ground. "I can't believe we fell into another trap!"

"And the trap-maker split!" Spade added.

"What do you mean?" Ben asked, sitting up.

"The person who pushed you ran out of the shack and hopped into a red van. They're gone. Splitsville!"

Maya stood up. "Come on, Ben. Let's get out of here."

A few minutes later Maya and Ben were sitting

in the bus, dejected. Not only had they missed the agent, but they were left without a clue as to where to go next.

"Would some pear pancakes cheer you up?" Ben asked.

"I thought you said they sounded weird," Maya said.

"I did," Ben replied. "But I don't know what else to do, and right now pancakes sound like the best thing to me."

A little while later the bus pulled up in front of the restaurant that Maya had visited with her aunt years before. They settled into a cozy booth and the waitress came over.

"Can I take your order?" she asked.

"Pear pancakes," said Maya.

"I don't like pears," said Ben. "Can I get . . . watermelon pancakes?"

"Watermelon pancakes?" the waitress said. "That's the second odd order I got today."

"What was the other odd order you received today?" Ben wanted to know.

"A tofu burger, hold the onions, and a low-fat vegetable shake to go," the waitress answered.

"Sounds like your customer was on a diet," Ben said.

The waitress shrugged again. "The person was strange, that's for sure. Couldn't even tell if they were male or female, with those dark glasses and coat and hat."

Dark glasses, a coat, and a hat? Could it be?

"Did you notice anything else about this customer? Did he or she say anything else?" Maya asked.

The waitress shook her head. "Nope." Then she walked away to place their order.

"It's too bad," said Maya. "That information doesn't help. *Both* of our suspects eat dietetic food."

Ben sighed and stared off into space. What was it about onions that seemed so familiar? He furrowed his brow in concentration. Suddenly it came to him.

"That's it!" Ben shouted.

"What's it?" Maya asked.

"Hammond Swiss's terrible breath," Ben said.

"Who could forget that?" said Maya. "He almost knocked me out when we arrested him last time."

"Well," said Ben, "he had bad breath because he ate anchovies, garlic, and *onions*."

"Onions?" Maya said. "But the waitress said

that the customer ordered a tofu burger with no onions. That means there's only one suspect left—Polly Graph!"

"Let's call Wanda for a warrant," Ben said.

The waitress came back with their order. "There was one thing I forgot," she said. "That customer kept on calling me 'Babe' and laughing. Then they asked me if I got bunions on my feet from standing so much. Strange, very strange," the waitress said, walking away.

"That has to be some sort of clue," Ben said. He whipped out the Ultra-Secret Sender.

Maya opened up the roadside-attractions guidebook. "What do the words *babe* and *bunion* have in common?" she asked. She furrowed her brow in concentration. "Baby feet? Hold the bunions? Hey, I got it!" she shouted. "Paul Bunyan and his blue ox, Babe. And they can be found in a place called the Trees of Mystery in Klamath, California."

"All right, Maya!" Ben shouted. "And since it's Day Seven, that must be the final rendezvous with Carmen. We've got to move!"

"Waitress!" Maya shouted. "We need these pancakes to go. And fast!"

Back on the bus again, Dusty informed Maya

and Ben that Klamath was about a hundred-mile drive away. She knew some back roads that would lead them right there.

Maya and Ben were very excited that they were on their way to catch Polly Graph and Carmen. But they were nervous, too. Carmen's deadline was coming near, and they had no time to spare.

"What if we miss them?" Ben asked.

"If we miss them, we're doomed either way," Maya said. "Doomed because Carmen will have Interstate Eighty, and doomed because The Chief will have to join Carmen if we ever want the road back again. But let's not think about that." She shuddered.

"Well, this Trees of Mystery Place sounds really cool," Ben said as he picked up a printout from the Ultra-Secret Sender.

"It's located in Redwood National Park. 'The park preserves twenty-eight thousand acres of coastal redwoods and their environments. The Trees of Mystery are located near the mouth of the Klamath River, which is California's second-largest river. The river is home to king salmon, steelhead trout, perch, sturgeon, and flounder,'" Ben read aloud.

"And there's probably tons of water sports

there," Maya added. "And camping, too."

Ben nodded and sighed. "Sounds like a great vacation spot."

Before they knew, it, Dusty pulled the bus into the parking lot for the Trees of Mystery.

"Check it out, dudes!" Dusty said. "The elusive red van!"

"I wonder why Polly parked it in plain sight," Ben said.

"Because this is the end of the road!" Maya said excitedly. "Dusty, you stay by the red van in case Polly comes back. We'll explore the redwoods. Let's go!"

Maya and Ben ran to the entrance. A forty-nine-foot-tall statue of Paul Bunyan and Babe the Blue Ox stood guard.

"Well, hello there, little girl . . . ever see a fella as big as me?" a loud voice said.

"Wh-what was that?" Maya said, jumping backward.

Ben laughed. "It was just our friend Paul here, welcoming us. What's the matter, Maya, feeling a little jittery?"

"It just startled me, that's all," Maya said, angry at herself for letting something so silly scare her. "Come on, Ben. Let's go. We're wasting time!"

The forest trail began at a giant fake hollow redwood log.

"I hope this place isn't just one big tourist trap. . . . Whoa!" Maya exclaimed. "Check it out!"

Soaring redwood trees surrounded her. Some shot up straight to the sky; others grew at crazy angles.

"This place is great!" Ben said.

"And big," Maya said. "We'd better split up." She reached into her backpack and pulled out two whistles, then handed one to Ben. "If you see Polly or Carmen, give the whistle three short blows. And keep doing it at three-second intervals. I'll do the same," she explained. "You go to the left, and I'll go to the right."

Ben nodded. "Good luck." And he ran off.

Ben couldn't believe the fantastic forms the trees in the forest took. There were trees shaped like pretzels, and DNA helixes. There was the Cathedral Tree, which consisted of nine living trees growing from one root structure, and the Family Tree, which was twelve trees growing from one trunk of a Sitka spruce—thirty-two feet in circumference. Also on the trail were animals, like a huge bear and a bear cub, carved in redwood with a chain saw.

Ben looked high up into the trees. He peeked behind branches and shrubs. He even walked around and around the huge tree trunks and peered inside hollow trees. But no Polly. And no Carmen.

Just as Ben was about to give up, something caught his eye. A flash of red up in a tree! Quickly, Ben pulled out his whistle and gave three short blows. He ran over to the tree. It was the Candelabra Tree—a long trunk lying across the road, with several tall redwoods growing straight from its trunk.

Ben blew the whistle again. Where was Maya? Then Ben saw Polly Graph climbing one of the trees. She was holding on to a small black box.

"Polly Graph!" Ben shouted. "I have a warrant for your arrest. Come down here immediately!"

Polly Graph laughed. "Sure! As soon as I deliver this little package!"

Suddenly Ben heard the sound of whirring blades. He looked up and saw a red helicopter. A long rope ladder dangled from it, and a woman in red hung on.

It was Carmen Sandiego! "Stop, thief!" Ben cried.

Ben blew the whistle again, but there was no sign of Maya. He would have to handle this alone.

Ben boosted himself up on the tree trunk that was lying across the road. He looked up. The helicopter was moving Carmen closer to Polly! Ben grabbed one of the upright tree trunks and tried to climb up. But there was nothing to hold on to, and he slid down.

What am I going to do? Ben asked himself. *I've got to stop them!* He blew his whistle again. Suddenly Ben heard a cry from up above. It was Polly. The little black box fell from her hands, toward the ground. Quickly Ben sprang into action. Not taking his eyes off the box, he leaped forward and caught it!

Just then Ben heard a whistle blow. It sounded like it was coming from the tree. It was Maya! Somehow she had climbed up the tree and caught Polly.

"Maya!" Ben called, "catch Carmen!"

"Carmen Sandiego!" Maya shouted. "You're under arrest!"

"Not this time, clever child!" Carmen shouted, hovering over Maya's head. "You may have gotten my agent and my little box, but not me!"

"That's what you think!" Maya shouted. And with that, she leaped up and grabbed Carmen's feet.

"Maya!" Ben shouted. "Have you gone crazy? Come back!"

But it was too late. The helicopter lifted up, carrying Carmen, and Maya with her!

13
San Francisco, California

"What do you think you're doing?" Carmen called to Maya.

"I'm bringing you in," Maya replied.

"And how are you going to do that?" Carmen wanted to know. "This is *my* helicopter you're hanging on."

She's got a point, Maya thought.

"Besides," Carmen continued, "my little game is over. You will return Interstate Eighty to its rightful place, and you get to keep your beloved Chief. What else do you want?"

"You!" Maya shouted. The ladder began to sway, and they were pulled higher and higher. They were above the tallest redwoods.

"Maya!" Maya heard Ben call. "Come down! You're going to get killed!"

"Carmen Sandiego, you are under arrest!" Maya said. She reached into her pocket for her handcuffs—and lost her grip! She began plummeting to the ground.

Ben gasped. "Oh, no!" he shouted. He didn't want to watch, but he couldn't take his eyes off his friend. Down, down she fell; then she pulled a cord on her backpack. She floated to the ground safely.

Good thing ACME just came up with these mini-parachutes! she said to herself as she stood up.

"I'll get The Chief next time! Don't you worry!" she heard Carmen call as she flew away.

Ben walked over. "You had me scared there for a minute," he said to Maya. "That backpack came in handy once again!"

Maya looked up and saw Polly climbing down the tree. "Hurry up, Polly," she called.

"You've got guts, kid," Polly said grudgingly. "I'm all yours."

A few minutes later Polly joined Maya and Ben on the ground.

"I can't believe Carmen got away! I was so close!" Maya said.

"Well, at least we got our henchperson," Ben said. "Now tell us what's in this box." He held the black box in front of Polly.

"Your little road!" Polly said with a laugh.

"What?" Maya and Ben said together.

"You heard me," Polly said. "Your road, Interstate Eighty."

"How did you get it to fit in there?" Ben asked.

"Easy. With this little Matter Pulverizing Ray Gun," Polly said, pulling a small black gun out of her pocket.

"Don't point that thing in our direction," Maya said nervously.

"And why not?" Polly asked. "With one pull of the trigger, all forms of matter pulverize into tiny molecules—small enough to carry in a box that size," she explained, pointing at the box. "And to get it back to its original form, all I have to do is press the reverse button. Clever, but very dangerous! Now, let's see if it works on humans. You'll be microscopic in no time!"

"Don't do it, Polly!" Maya cried out.

As Polly pointed the gun at Maya, Ben sprang into action. He picked up a fallen branch from the ground and whacked the gun out of Polly's hand. Then, before Polly could react, he dove to the ground and picked up the gun.

"Now we've got you!" Ben said. "Polly Graph, you're officially under arrest!"

"Good work, gumshoes!" The Chief said. Maya and Ben were sitting in her office at ACME Headquarters.

"You had me worried for a while, but I had confidence that you'd pull through," The Chief said.

"So did we," Maya said.

"When were you sure that Polly Graph was the henchperson?" The Chief wanted to know.

"It wasn't until we picked up the final clue in the restaurant in Oregon," Maya explained. "And Polly finally admitted to us that she was purposely trying to make us think the henchperson was Hammond Swiss. She said she never liked him—she always found him too loud and boisterous!"

The Chief laughed. "Well, at least she's in custody now. As for Carmen, well . . ." She sighed.

"Maya was close, Chief. Real close," Ben said.

"I know what you did, Maya," The Chief said.

"And I'm really glad you're safe."

"Me too," Maya said. "Me too."

"And we also returned Interstate Eighty," Ben said. "You should have seen those travelers' expressions when the road materialized before their eyes. It was unbelievable!"

"Well, at least now people can go on their vacations," Maya added.

"Speaking of vacations," The Chief said, "I think you two deserve one. I'm sending you two on an all-expense paid trip to Wonder World!"

"All right!" said Ben. "I'll be a surfer dude yet!"

"Thanks, Chief!" Maya said.

"And a close friend of yours will be escorting you there," The Chief said, pointing at the door.

Maya and Ben turned around, and in walked Dusty.

"Not another bus ride, Chief," Ben groaned. "I don't think I can take it!"

The Chief gave him a stern look.

"I don't mean to be ungrateful or anything, it's just that—"

"Pipe down, dude," Dusty said. "Didn't I tell you that I have my pilot's license? I needed it when I was touring with the Flying Franks. They just hated to ride in cars."

"After this past week, so do we!" Maya laughed.

"Well, what are you waiting for?" Dusty asked. "Let's hit the sky!"